SPEAK, SEÑOR REYNOLDS—

"Tell me, Reynolds," the Dictator said, "aren't you pro-Communist? A bit of a fellow traveler, say?"

"No."

"Why not?"

"Because they push people around."

The Dictator laughed. Pleasantly. Wholeheartedly. "And that, of course, is a terrible crime?"

"The most terrible," Peter answered. "Too hard to stop. Starts with a few broken heads in Munich. And ends up in Dachau...."

The Dictator drew in on his cigar. Studied Peter. "And what, my dear Peter Reynolds, do you think of *my* government?"

Peter smiled. "I'd rather not say."

"Why not?" The two words were a whipcrack.

Peter smiled, even more slowly, "Because there are ladies present!"

———

THE OLD GODS LAUGH
was originally published
by The Dial Press.

THE
OLD GODS
LAUGH

Frank Yerby

 A POCKET CARDINAL® EDITION published by
POCKET BOOKS, INC. • NEW YORK

THE OLD GODS LAUGH

Dial Press edition published June, 1964

A Pocket *Cardinal* edition
1st printing.........March, 1965

**This Pocket *Cardinal*® edition includes every word contained in the
original, higher-priced edition. It is printed from brand-new
plates made from completely reset, clear, easy-to-read type.
Pocket *Cardinal* editions are published by Pocket Books, Inc.,
and are printed and distributed in the U.S.A. by Affiliated Publishers,
a division of Pocket Books, Inc., 630 Fifth Avenue, New York, N.Y. 10020.
Trademarks registered in the United States and other countries.**

L

FIRST NOTE TO THE READER

The writer sincerely hopes that no earnest reader will confuse the very real Republica de Costa Verde with those imaginary ones found on the maps of the geography books, scattered in multicolored profusion around seas of pale blue ink. Nor attempt to identify Miguel Villalonga with any of the swart, pudgy little strong men who have no being a priori in the Kantian, Hegelian sense, since we know them only a posteriori as created by those wonderful novelists, the Dostoevskis of the Public Press.

To continue this customary disclaimer: Peter Reynolds, Judith Lovell, Alicia Villalonga, Isabela de los Cienmilamores, Luis Sinnombre, Padre Pío, Tim O'Rourke, Jacinto of the Yellow Eyes, and the rest, of course resemble many people living or dead, with this difference: They are alive, while the persons to whom they may seem to have certain similarities, and you, Reader, and I—

  . . . Are such stuff
As dreams are made on, and our little life
Is rounded with a sleep.

SECOND NOTE TO THE READER

I have called this book a Modern Romance. Exactly what I mean by that, I do not know; except, perhaps, that it is *not* a realistic novel; and is hopefully dedicated to the old-fashioned reader, who reads for fun.

Madrid
December, 1963

Two Somewhat Irrelevant Quotations

Inside that mountain
My Lord spoke,
Out of that mountain
Came fire and smoke. . . .
—Negro spiritual

The Gods are dead. They all died laughing
the day when one old Grim Beard of a God
got up and said: "Thou shalt have no other
Gods before me."
—Nietzsche, *Thus Spake Zarathustra*

Book One

THE MOUNTAINS

1.

The wind came in from the sea so that the plume of smoke that had not left the top of Zopocomapetl for five years now bent inland above the tropical rainforest, and Peter could see the town. It was very white. The houses were hard-edged and clear even from where they rode, picking their way across the long slant of solidified lava seven hundred meters down from the snowline, and fifteen hundred, more or less, above Ciudad Villalonga. Except on the eastern side, the part of the town nearest the sea. There the heat waves coming up from the burning oil refinery the Castristas had dynamited the night before made the houses dance like stones seen under moving water. The sooty, black-capped orange flames stood straight up for two hundred meters. Then the wind took them, too, bending them over in the same direction as the smoke from the volcano, driving them westward toward the Sierras Nevadas, white-peaked and mist-blue beyond the town.

"I have heard," the guide said, "that the oil company is flying a man down from Texas to put out the fire. An expert in this business of putting out oil fires. They spend uselessly both their money and his time. Tomorrow, the exalted ones who would import the revolution from Cuba, whiskers and all, for our special benefit, will only start another fire. A bigger one."

3

"Then you are not of the Castristas, Tomas?" Peter said.

"*Hombre*—" Tomas said, "so much as that—no———"

"But neither are you for The Unconquerable, The Generous Benefactor of the people of the Glorious Republic of Costa Verde, The Father of the Country, The Supreme Head of the Everlasting State?"

The guide Tomas looked around him in every direction. At this level—because they were newly made and the wind hadn't had time to sculpture them—the slopes were gentle. They had been flattened by the lava flow from the last major eruption, the one that had buried the Pueblo of Chitimaya up to the bell tower of the church. On the surface of the slope lay a foot or two of volcanic ash. The horses hoofs sank into the ash. Sometimes they broke through the top crust of the lava, too, and the smoke came up around them. When that happened, the horses would snort and roll their eyes, and dance. The guide had warned Peter to expect that before they had started out. It was only a matter of holding the big-barreled, short-legged, shaggy mountain ponies hard between their knees and sawing at their tough mouths with the bits until they stopped it. Which didn't even call for thinking after the first time. But there was no vegetation at all, except here and there a clump of those white flowers that the Indians called La Flor de la Muerte, The Flower of Death. The flowers were very beautiful, but they weren't tall enough or thick enough for a man to hide behind. While he was waiting for Tomas to reassure himself of that fact, Peter Reynolds looked out over the white town to the bay where the two aircraft carriers, one British, one American, waited to take their respective nationals off, in case the revolution got beyond the stage of random bombings and nightly murders. The *Seaflower*, The Leader's yacht, wasn't in the bay at all.

The guide looked at Peter. What he was trying to make his mind up about now was another thing.

"Señor Reporter," he said, "is it your custom to write in your newspaper all things which are said to you?"

"Yes," Peter said. "But never the names or even the professions of those who say them in countries like yours, or in troubled times like these. It would pain me much to think that your teeth, your blood, and pieces of your skin might be splattered over the walls of one of The Unconquerable's Centers of Moral Correction and Social Re-education because of an indiscretion of mine. Hence I do not commit such indiscretions. Of that you can be secure."

"Good," Tomas said. "Then I will say it, since it is a thing which, if you have been down here even a day, you already know: Nobody is for Villalonga. Not even his great whore of a mother. Last week at a party at the embassy of your country, she said that if she knew with any certainty who the father of Miguel was, she would emasculate him to make sure he begat no more monsters. Of course she had been drinking the whiskey of your country to which she is unaccustomed. Someone who knew her in the days of her glory— when she was the star of those curious exhibitions performed at La Luna Azul, in which intervened men, women, creatures of indeterminate sex, horses, dogs, and even monkeys— remarked that to have any certainty she would have to geld the entire male population of Costa Verde above the age of fifty, in which the Castrated would outnumber the Castristas."

"And from then on could be distinguished from them by their lack of beards," Peter said.

"Aiyi!" Tomas laughed. "You extend the jest. I must remember that—"

They looked down at the city.

"Señor Reynolds—" the guide said.

"Yes, Tomas?"

"If this of the Fidelistas goes badly, what am I to tell Señorita Lovell?"

Peter looked at him. Said:

"The same thing I told her before we left: 'Gringa, go home!'"

"I do not understand this. You, Señor, it seems to me, are the luckiest of men, and . . ."

"Luck is various," Peter said. "There is the luck of winning a million pesos in the National Lottery; but also the luck of keeping them, once won. Or, to put it another way: You were once, in your youth, a killer of bulls, no?"

"No," Tomas said, "that is a lie I tell to the usual type of tourists. But since you are neither a tourist, and certainly not ordinary, speaking, as you do, our language like a Spaniard of Spain . . ."

"Which is where I learned it," Peter said.

"I find myself compelled to the truth. A rarity, no? I was a peon in the *cuatela* of the great Manuel. Manuel the Mighty. So I can talk convincingly of the bulls. I have, after all, run them. I was not bad with the cape. With the *banderillas*, excellent. It is probable that I would have become a torero if I had not been gored. But fear entered me along with the horn of that black enormity from Piedras Negras. Much fear. More than I could dominate. So I quit. But what has this to do with Señorita Lovell? *Dios mío!* How pretty she is! No, more than pretty—beautiful in truth! Why——"

"So," Peter said, "are those flowers over there."

Tomas looked at Peter.

"Do you know what they are called, Señor?" he said.

"Yes," Peter said, "The Flowers of Death."

Tomas went on looking at him.

"Many times I have had difficulty understanding the people of your country," he said, "but that was because my English is bad; or in the few cases where they believed themselves capable of speaking Spanish, what they spoke was of an incomprehensibility total. But with you, there does not exist this difficulty. What you say is perfectly clear. It is your meaning that is obscure."

"Perhaps I have no meaning," Peter said. "Perhaps there is no such thing. I sometimes think there isn't."

"*A iyai yai!*" the guide said. "Now you have lost me, truly. We were speaking of Señorita Lovell."

"No," Peter said, "we were speaking of luck. If that exists, either."

"*Sí, sí!* Clearly it exists! A man who can take nightly in his arms this blonde one with hair like sun on snow; eyes like those great blue flowers that open only in the morning; lips like . . ."

"Let us not enter into details over all the physical excellences of the Señorita Lovell. Nor indulge in speculations about the precise nature of my relations with her. I grant you that a man who knows her within any of the acceptable degrees of intimacy is lucky, surely. And when he speaks against luck, he blasphemes, no? But I do not speak against it, Amigo. I simply say it is various. That there is—say the luck of placing the *banderillas* side by side in the great hump of muscle that grows behind the bull's neck—power to power, you call that one, don't you? And the bad luck of having them fall out, once placed. There is the fine luck of killing cleanly with one enormous sword thrust; or dying well against the planks of the *barrera* with the horn in your guts and all the lovely girls screaming in horror and in anguish as you die, going out on the great wave of their wail of self-pity, for it is that, you know, Friend Tomas, because they individually and collectively have lost in a very personal manner all that maleness, all that valor, even—though they know it not—the sweet, night-long use of that mighty pair which gave you what it took to do this thing. But there is also the luck of living on after a horn wound of the gravest kind, when that hard black living spike destroys the femoral artery or enters between the cheeks of the buttocks. One lives on, after a fashion; but belly, groin, and thigh look like the map of Costa Verde, and all the natural functions are impaired—"

"You mean?" Tomas said.

"Nothing. Or everything. I knew Señorita Judith Lovell before. When she was nineteen years old and had played no more than secondary roles in minor Class B films. And again, five years ago, when she was twenty-two. In Madrid, where she was making the great spectacle picture about the Byzantine Empress Theodora. By then she was already between husbands, having divorced the first one and not yet acquired the second. Which might account for it. But then, it might not. Who knows?"

"What, Señor?" the guide said.

"*Hombre*, I talk to myself, posing questions which have no answers. But no questions have answers, truly, do they? And there are no solutions to anything whatsoever in this world. Which is enough of this subject. More than enough. A repletion."

"As the Señor wills. Shall we go, then? It is still far to the place where casually, accidentally, and unfortunately, you take the wrong fork of the trail and lose yourself—"

"And you," Peter said, "what will you do then?"

"Report the unfortunate occurrence to the authorities, who will then immediately publish a report that the celebrated North American journalist, Mr. Peter Reynolds, has been abducted by the Castristas and is probably undergoing torture, in order to induce your Marines to land and your Navy to send the planes from those aircraft carriers out there to bomb and machine-gun the jungles at the foot of the Sierras."

"You mean Villalonga *wants* us to send in the Marines?"

"Naturally. Who else would be willing to save his hide? You North Americans are a strange people. You call yourselves democratic, and yet you support the enemies of the people, everywhere—"

"Say we support the less dangerous of the people's enemies against the more," Peter said. "Is there not in Spanish a proverb which goes 'Better the known evil than the unknown good'?"

" '*Mejor lo malo conocido que lo bueno por conocer . . .*'? *Sí*. We say that, yes. But in the case of Miguel Villalonga, the proverb is without meaning. For nothing could be worse than Villalonga. Nothing at all."

"You've got a point there," Peter said. "Come. Let us ride on while there is still light."

Now where they rode it was cold and the wind came down from the snow-capped peak of Zopocomapetl with a sting of fine flakes, and something else, too—they did not know what it was until they came around the shoulder of the volcano to the side where the lava spilled over the rim and melted the snow. Then the horses began to snort and buck;

looking at Tomas, Peter saw the guide was crying blood. He put his hand to his own cheeks and his fingers came away sticky and red, but he saw it was a kind of wet red mud, mixed with steam vapor and the mist from the melting snow. They both started coughing at the same time, doubled over in the saddle while the vapor that was nearly three parts pure sulphuric acid to seven parts steam tore into them. The guide jerked his pony's head around, and they went down the slope very fast on the edge of the fresh lava flow that was too hot to cross, being cherry-red and blistering their foreheads above the snow goggles they had put on, even from five meters away.

When they were out of it and picking their way across the lower tongue of solidified lava that wasn't always even solid but was always so hot that getting across the narrowest part, twenty-five meters wide, was an exercise in horsemanship, they stopped and washed their faces in the rivulets of melted snow.

"Can one drink it?" Peter said.

"No," the guide said. "It is, like the smoke, of a poisonous nature. Better to use the water in the canteens."

Peter unslung his canteen, drank, but rolled the water around in his mouth without swallowing it. When he spat it out, it looked like blood, and some of it maybe was, the acid vapor had burned his throat so. But it made him feel better.

"Now," Tomas said, "we are past the bad part. From here on, it is all downward."

"Is this where I leave you?"

"No; not yet. In that place there is a definite fork in the trail which makes this of your getting lost plausible in case Our Glorious Leader investigates. Señor Reynolds, will you explain something to me? I do not mean to put my nostrils into your business, but I should be happier if I understood——"

"Understood what?" Peter asked.

"This of Padre Pío. What interest has your paper in saving him?"

Peter looked at the guide.

"You think he's alive?" he said.

"I know he is alive. The Castristas are not so stupid as to murder him. For, by doing that, they would lose surely what they hope to gain."

"Which is?" asked Peter.

"The Indians. You know that seventy-five per cent of the population of Costa Verde is of pure Indian race. Without them, the revolution has no chance. Yet so far, peons that they are, hungry, abused, almost slaves, with nothing to lose and everything to gain, they have not joined it."

"Because of Padre Pío?"

"Because of Padre Pío. And because they love the little brown Indian Virgin, and the Saints with the faces of Tluscolas he caused to be painted. Because they are by nature devout. You know they worship their ancestors and the dead? Until Padre Pío induced them to accept Christian burial, they used to keep their dead in a room with barred windows to keep the pumas and the wolves out, until they mummified. Then they would sit them at the table with the living at every meal, and do them honor, offering the first and the best of the maize and the goat meat and the *mescal* to them—"

"That must help the appetite," Peter said.

"It is macabre," Tomas said, "but it is also beautiful. Piety always is, no matter what its nature . . ."

"So the reason the Communists kidnapped Padre Pío is—?"

"To induce him to stop telling the Indians that the first thing they would do upon gaining the power would be to burn all the churches as they did in Spain."

"And how do they propose to induce him to do this? By pulling out his fingernails?"

"No, Señor. I have told you they are not stupid. They seek to make a bargain with him. It is said they propose to make him Archbishop of the State Church when they come to power."

"And he?"

"Is neither stupid nor for sale. He says that of cowardly archbishops of captive churches there is already an excess, that what is necessary in this world is faith, and the valor

to die for it if need be. Besides, he says they are incapable
of realizing that his priesthood detracts not one jot from his
Spanish manhood but rather adds to it."

"Spanish manhood?" Peter said. "He is Spanish, then, your
Padre Pío?"

"Vasco. Basque. Which is the same. Only stubborner."

"You," Peter said, "have much precise and detailed information on this matter, no, Amigo?"

Tomas shrugged.

"I am a guide," he said. "I go many places. And my hearing is of a sufficient keenness. Besides, when one has lived
the number of years that I have under the rule of the Generous Benefactor of the People of Costa Verde, one automatically closes one's mouth to preserve one's teeth. With
the Fidelites, I am a Red; with the Army officers, who alone
support our Leader because they know that upon the day of
the uprising the people will lynch them along with the Generous Benefactor and with equal justice, I am more rightist
than Villalonga himself. Here it is only by being all things
to all men that one stays alive."

"Yet Padre Pío—"

"Is safe from both sides, because his death at the hands of
either would mean the ruin of their hopes. Now here we
have a journalist! I ask him a question, which not only does
he not answer, but in recompense for my impertinence in
asking it, he digs out of me the replies to ten questions of his
own. But I ask it still: Why, in a country of Protestants—"

"Like our President?" Peter said.

"All right. I will say it differently. Why, in a country with
a majority of Protestants, does a newspaper interest itself so
much in the fate of an obscure Basque priest?"

"There is not much news these days, Amigo. Or rather
there is too much. All of it of a boring sameness: 'Shall we
bomb them, or will they bomb us?' So this of the little Padre
Pío, with his faith, his valor, his Spanish manhood, his heart,
say. It tugs at the emotions—which, Amigo Tomas, is what
sells papers. And that's all I am—a paper boy. 'Wuxtra!
Read all about it! PARISH PRIEST DEFIES REDS!'"

The guide looked upward toward the cone of the volcano. Above it now the sky was red.

"I do not permit myself the luxury of criticism," he said, "but it seems to me ugly, this thing you have said."

"What isn't?" Peter said. "In my lifetime, and yours, Friend, what hasn't been?"

And now, having passed that fork, he was alone. The trail went down very steeply, and the coolness went out of the air. In a little while he was going to be down to the level where the jungle growth started. He knew what that was like. He had been in tropical rainforest before. So he stopped where he was and made camp for the night. Here it was still cool enough for him to sleep comfortably. He was still above the level of the insects that came in stinging clouds and ate a man alive, above the height favored by the vampire bats, the scorpions and the snakes. He slept very well, being awakened only once by a puma who was trying to get at the horse. He shot at the puma with his carbine and missed it, but it went away. Farther down in the jungle it might have been a jaguar instead of a puma. And missing *el tigre*, as the Indios called the jaguar, would have been fatal. He cursed himself for a rotten shot, and went back to sleep.

One hour after he'd started out the next morning, half an hour from his prearranged place of rendezvous with the Castroites, Fidelites, Communoids, he saw the plane.

It was so high up that all he could make out about it was that it was a high-winged monoplane with gear that didn't retract. But even from that height they must have spotted him, because the next time it appeared it was only three hundred meters up and he could not only recognize the type but also read the markings. A Piper Cub, Civilian. Registered in Costa Verde itself. It lifted, went away. But when he hauled the mule-stubborn mountain pony around the next bend of the trail, it met him head on in a classic strafing run so low that the spinning sunlit disk of the propeller was directly in front of him, and he could see the pilot's eyes. But he kept on riding upright, not throwing himself out of the saddle as the pilot probably wanted him to, until the rate of closure was a sickening thing and even the sound of the eighty-five horsepower double-opposed Lycoming was no louder than the beating of his heart. It rose a little, lazily, negligently, went over at a distance so close that if he had had a knife in his hand he could easily have punctured one of the fat, low-pressure tires.

For the next half minute he couldn't see where it had gone; he was too busy trying to stay on the horse, amid the little tornado of volcanic ash and dust the prop had kicked up. By the time he had the beast quieted the Cub came over again, climbing now, and flew straight ahead of him in the direction he was going. Three kilometers away, or maybe five, it circled once, twice, three times. Then it went up again, headed back toward Ciudad Villalonga, climbing all the time; but when it got to Zopocomapetl it still wasn't high enough, so it banked vertically around the rim of the volcano just under the smoke. After that he couldn't see it any more.

Three and a half kilometers down the trail, he met the Communist guerrillas.

They came out of the woods on both sides of the trail. They had Czech-made machine pistols in their hands. The pistols had a twenty-five shot clip that stuck horizontally from the side of the gun, and slotted air-cooled barrels. They also had a rifle stock that was nothing more than an open lightweight metal frame that clipped into the back of the pistol grip so the gun could be raised to the shoulder and sighted like a rifle. But none of them was even starting to pull the damnfool trick of trying to aim one of those little squirters. They'd found out, or had been taught long ago, that holding the stock of a burp gun to your shoulder while in a standing position and trying to draw a bead on your target through the rudimentary notched sights had three absolutely certain results: The recoil raised the muzzle until you were spraying the treetops; the blowtorch spluttering blast at the muzzle thirty scant centimeters in front of your eyes left you blinder than a bat; and that nice, pretty, all-but-useless stock slammed back against your shoulder in a series of mule kicks that broke your collarbone. From the easy way they held those lethally beautiful lightweight assault arms— hip high, cradled against one side, the muzzle pulled down low by the left hand on the forward grip, ready to swing in a flat, belly-ripping arc, Peter could see that some Red Army drill sergeant on the Island of Cuba had known his business forward, backward, and crosswise.

They were all very young. They all wore beards. They were all dressed in paratroopers' uniforms without insignia. Jungle uniforms, spotted with camouflage.

"*Hola,*" Peter said.

They didn't answer him. They stood there looking at him with the two eyes in their heads, and those other great dark final eyes that were the muzzles of the burp guns.

"*Buenas días,*" Peter said. "My name is—"

"We know who you are," the tallest one, clearly their leader, said.

"Look, Juan!" the second one said. "Kill him. There is no doubt possible. Or permit me that I do it, myself. Because, if not—"

"Shut up," snapped the one called Juan. "I give the orders."

The other said nothing. Peter noted that the one who had no possible doubt and wanted Juan to kill him had yellow eyes. They looked like the eyes of the puma he'd shot at and missed the night before.

"Señor Reynolds," Juan said. "You will throw down your carbine to the ground. Slowly. Without abrupt movements."

Peter eased the Winchester out of its saddle sheath, let it trail downward until the muzzle was almost touching the ground. Then he let go of it. The thud it made striking the earth didn't carry too far.

"Now your revolver."

"I have no revolver," Peter said.

Juan nodded. Yellow Eyes stepped up to the horse and ran his hands all over Peter, stepped back.

"He has no pistol, Chief," he said.

"All right," Juan said. "Now, Señor North American Journalist, you will dismount, remove your radio very carefully from your pack and hand it to Jacinto, here." When he said that he nodded a little in the direction of the one with the yellow eyes.

Peter swung down off the shaggy pony, stood there looking at them.

"Señor Jefe—" he said.

"Camarada Jefe," Juan said.

"Comrade Chief," Peter said, "I am of those who have no spiritual affinity with the twentieth century. Revolvers in my hand, refuse to shoot. Radios always have their batteries dead. Therefore I dispense with them, and with all things I am incapable of managing—"

"You lie!" Jacinto of the yellow eyes said.

"Shut up, Jacinto," Juan said. Then to Peter: "Your radio, Reynolds. Your walkie-talkie. The small apparatus with which you summoned that plane."

"I am here," Peter said. "There is my horse. You have many hands, all of which need not be occupied with those little machine guns. So find it, this marvelous radio of the black novels of espionage with which I have communicated with the air force of a man for whom I have no use at all."

"Why not?" Juan said. "Why have you no use for our sweet little Fascist?"

"I have a big nose. And a weak stomach. A bad combination, no? Say I object to Miguelito's smell."

"And how does he smell, Comrade Reporter?" Juan said.

"Of death," Peter said.

Juan stood there, looking at Peter. Then he turned to Jacinto.

"Search him," he ordered; "search the horse."

"He has no radio, either," Jacinto said, "at least, not now."

"What do you think I did with it, if I don't have it now?" Peter said. "Swallow it?"

"No," Jacinto said. "For that even an apparatus of transistors would be too big. You threw it, doubtless, into the brush before meeting us here. From the time the little aircraft descended close enough to touch your head until you reached us, you had time enough for that. We could not keep you in sight every moment."

"From here to there is three kilometers," Peter said, "all of it but the last hundred meters bare rock and volcanic ash. My beautiful radio will be in plain sight beside the road. I could not throw it far. I am not strong enough. Here, take my horse and go to get it. I am longing to have my radio back. I miss it. I want to call the White House. Tell our Irish President not to worry. That he need only shoot off a fire-cracker, and enemies of such imagination will die of heart attacks, thinking it the H bomb."

"A comic," Jacinto said. "A clown. But a clown of the bad death, making jokes of a fatal lack of humor. Jefe, with your permission I will make him another mouth—a little farther down, about the level of his windpipe, say. So that he may laugh out of them both . . ."

"Leave him in peace," Juan said. "He threw down nothing after this of the little plane. I was watching him through the glasses. Yet that pilot dived upon him like a hawk. Tell me, Comrade Reporter, how do you explain that?"

"I cannot explain it," Peter said. "I can only speculate."

"Speculate then," Juan said.

"I think that an officer of the Security Police must have been present in the saloon of The Blue Moon when I made the arrangements to ransom Padre Pío. In civilian clothes, of course. Or that one or more of the *chicas* there sells information as well as her perfumed flesh. From getting that information to hanging a tail on me was just a step. You will note that they did not send a big and powerful aircraft loaded with bombs and machine guns to wipe you out once I had located you and called them with the radio I do not have. Instead they sent that little yellow toy of an airplane which can fly almost as slowly as a horse walks and hence is useful in locating a single rider on a mountain trail. But this, I think, has no importance now. What does have importance is that we all leave this place with a certain rapidity."

"Why?" said Jacinto.

"Because, Comrade, while I admit that this skin my sainted mother gave me is no longer handsome, after having been burned and stung by thirty-seven years of sun and wind, and having been perforated with various metallic objects in various wars, the fact remains it is the only skin I have and I retain a kind of sentimental fondness for it. My desire to preserve it, more or less intact, is keen."

"I think," Jacinto said, in rare good humor now, "that the Comrade Reporter has nothing in his pants. And that he sits down to urinate."

"And I that you have nothing in your head," Juan said, "except your tongue, which is as loose and heavy as the clapper of a church bell—and just as meaningless."

He turned to Peter with a little smile.

"Shall we go, Comrade Reporter?"

They moved through the jungle on foot. Two of the soldiers went ahead, hacking out a trail with their machetes. Peter walked between Juan and Jacinto. All the rest, fourteen in all, followed. The last man led Peter's horse. He had taken advantage of the occasion to hang his machine pistol and his pack over the horn of the saddle so he didn't have to carry any weight through the brush.

It was hard going. Every plant had thorns. The insects rose up. The sound of their wing-drumming, long-tearing whine filled the heavy, hot, wet, stench-laden air. What little patches of sky were visible through the treetops, ominous and dark with the smoke from the volcano, they blotted out as they came down. They hit the horse first. He went crazy. Juan had to put another soldier at his head to help hold him down. Then they hit Peter. A hundred red-hot needles plunged into every visible, uncovered inch of his flesh.

"Here," Juan said. "Take this. Smear it over your face and arms."

This was an oily insect repellent. The insects loved it. They ate it up.

The lead guerrillas killed a python with their machetes. It

was bigger around than the biceps of a wrestler, and a shade over fourteen feet long.

"How," Peter asked, "do you stay in this place, Comrade Chief?"

"We don't," Juan said. "We only use it for cover on our raids. Do not preoccupy yourself, Comrade Reynolds. We shall be out of it, very soon . . ."

They were. Two hours later they came out of the jungle at the foot of the Sierras. Started up them. Before they had reached the three-hundred-meter level, Peter was freezing. The wind blew through his clothes. They were soaked with the sweat that hadn't been able to evaporate in the steam wash of the jungle. But even after they had blown dry, he kept on being cold. His teeth chattered. His lips were blue. Something was happening to his eyes. They wouldn't focus. Juan, Jacinto, the guerrillas ballooned and shrank, towered into giants, diminished into dwarfs, elongated into a multiple lizard with hundreds of feet. He saw that some of the feet had hoofs, and laughed aloud.

Juan looked at him. Turned to Jacinto.

"We halt here," he said. "Get out the medicines. Call Pepe. As a doctor he is not much; but since we have no other—"

The one called Pepe slipped the needle into his arm expertly. Then the three of them, Juan, Jacinto, and Pepe, squatted around him in a circle until he began to sweat. The water poured out of him in rivers. Then it slowed. Peter opened his eyes.

"How long was I out?" he said.

"Two hours," Juan said. "Comrade Reynolds, do you think you could stay in the saddle?"

"I think so," Peter said. "Why?"

"It is too exposed for us to make camp here. Especially since Villalonga is equipped with the airplanes given him by your government to aid him in his fight against the Communist Menace, the Red Threat, the Fidelista Infiltration—namely us—a sum total of less than a thousand men, scattered throughout the Sierras with nothing heavier than mortars to use against his tanks—"

"Castro had no more," Peter said, "but look at Cuba now."

Jacinto lifted up his head and laughed aloud. It wasn't a pleasant sound.

"What diverts you, Comrade?" Peter said.

"A jest. A good one. This medicine, Señor Don Hireling of the Bloodsucking Capitalist Press, which we used to break the onslaught of your fever is part of the ransom Fidel forced you to pay for the stupid and clumsy sons of the oppressors of the Cuban people we took while they were trying to play Commandos at the Bay of the Pigs!"

"You took?" Peter said. "You were there?"

"And Juan. And two or three of the others. We were getting our training in guerrilla tactics under our valiant Cuban brothers at the time."

"You mean under the Russians," Peter said.

"No," Juan said. "From them we learned only mountain warfare. They have no experience of jungle fighting. There are no jungles in Russia. That we learned from the Fidelistas themselves, who are past masters at it. Will you try to get up now?"

"Yes," Peter said, and got up. He felt their hands come out and take him, holding him until the trees, the sky, the mountains stopped their slow and stately dance above his head. Stood still again. Rock-solid, there.

Jacinto was still laughing.

"Tell me, Comrade Reporter," he said, "is it true that the invasion was planned by the infant daughter of your President? Or did the plans come to him in a sealed letter from the Pope in Rome?"

"No," Peter said. "I planned it for him. I'm good at that sort of thing."

Jacinto lifted his head and howled.

"What sort of thing, Comrade? Planning invasions?" Juan said.

"No. Screwing up the deal," Peter said.

He was dog-sick now, but he hung onto the saddle horn

with both hands. Juan came up to him. Gave him a canteen.
Said:

"Here—drink this. All you can."

It was dark Cuban rum. It flowed through his veins, making a warmth, a singing. He could feel his strength coming back. But he knew better than to trust that feeling. In the twelve years he'd worked the Latin American beat—with four out of the middle of them when he'd covered Spain, meeting Judith again there, learning some things about himself that weren't pleasant to contemplate even now—he knew how hard it was to get rid of tropical fevers. He knew he was in for it, that he could count on four or five days flat on his back, delirious, raving, and twenty days to three months of palsied, trembling, half-alive existence before he'd be able to shake off the effects.

He took another pull at the canteen. The sickness receded. He felt great.

"Think you can walk a little now?" Juan said. "This part will be difficult to manage on a horse."

"Of course I can walk," Peter said. "Another shot of that black glory, and I'll flap my wings and fly."

"Walking will be enough," Juan said.

Peter climbed down off the horse. He went on feeling fine. They went up the steep rocky trail. Ahead of them, Jacinto was still laughing.

Peter leaned close to Juan's ear.

"Is the Comrade Jacinto always entirely well in his mind?" he said.

"No," Juan said; "he is a little crazy. But it is a type of craziness which makes him a clever and dangerous fighter. Besides, he has reason enough to be mad."

"I see," Peter said.

They went on climbing. Now the effects of the rum were leaving him, and he was beginning to be sick again. But he hung on, alternately freezing and burning up, forcing his eyes to focus, his feet to move.

"We are almost there," Juan said. "You can see the sentries now."

Peter looked up just in time to see the sentries bringing the muzzles of their burp guns down and around in the direction of the trail. At once he threw himself flat on his belly.

Jacinto laughed aloud, clearly, gaily.

"As I told you," he said, "the foreigner sits down to—"

"Shut up!" Juan said; then he called out: "Point those unnameable namelessnesses of machine guns in another direction! And slowly. I have no wish to be murdered by the trembling hands of cowards. We come!"

The sentries swung the machine pistols away.

"Comrade Reynolds," Juan said.

Peter heard his name being called from a long way off. A very long way. But he didn't get up. It was very comfortable where he lay at the very heart of darkness, the nadir of existence—the warm, soft, lightless womb of time. Only Judith's face kept coming in, breaking the night apart. It was distorted, slack-lipped, her mouth a little opened, her breath stirring against his face. He heard her voice, but his mind rejected the words. She was being tender with him, after her own peculiar fashion. Which meant that everything she said was totally unprintable.

"Pick him up. We'll have to carry him in," Juan said.

2.

When he came back again it was morning and the sun was up, shining through the flap of the tent he was unaccountably in, and he was looking into an old man's face. The face was ugly. It was lined and seamed and crumpled and scarred until it looked like it had been accidentally eroded out of the bole of a tamarind tree by the sun and wind and decay and insects.

It was so ugly that Peter didn't believe it. For one thing, it had been there before, fading in and out of Judith's in the midst of that furious torture that she called making love. And he, knowing all the time that Judith wasn't there, that neither her face nor that Zopocomapetl lava bath consuming his loins was real, figured that this ancient gargoyle's face wasn't either. Only it was.

He lay there studying it with some care. Then it smiled at him and the ugliness was gone. Which was a rare thing. Somebody, something, somewhere flipped a switch and it was gone. Like the darkness goes when a light snaps on. In no time, no interval, without transition. And what was there now? Not beauty, but something finer. What there was in that face were all the words you couldn't say in English any more because English belonged to the twentieth century, to the age of anguish, and they sounded phony as all hell. But you could say them in Spanish because Spanish hadn't got out of the thirteenth century and maybe never would. All those big, fat, round, sonorous words ending in *dad; Tranquilidad. Serenidad. Bondad.* Even—hell, yes!—*Santidad.*

He kept on watching it, and the light came through the tent flap, and sculptured a body under it. A bent, wizened, old man's body, dressed in the cassock of a priest.

"Here we are!" the old man said. "By the grace of God and His infinite wisdom in permitting men to discover the wonders of His Science."

"Do not speak of God," Jacinto said. Turning on his cot, Peter saw him standing there in one corner of the tent, his young face, above the formless ink blot of his beard, orangered in the sunlight that filtered through the canvas. "God does not exist, Uncle Pío. He is a myth, invented by the capitalists to enslave the minds of the people with superstition."

"And you," Father Pío said, "you are a myth, Jacinto, invented by Karl Marx and distorted by Fidel Castro: That you are a handful of chemicals which can be bought for a few *reals*, a few kilos of insubstantial flesh on brittle bones, deterministically determined by some mindless glands and economic forces. Such a sad little myth, my son! How it diminishes you!"

"*Ha!*" Jacinto said. "Do not call me son, Priest! Do you know what a priest is, little Vasco?"

"Yes," Father Pío said. "A priest is a servant of God."

"A priest," Jacinto said, "is a man who is called father by all the world, except by his own children, who call him uncle."

"This is a jest, Jacinto?" Father Pío said. "Hmmn—not bad. I must remember it so that I can tell it to the Archbishop when I go back to Villalonga City."

"If you would listen to reason, you stubborn old fool, when you go back to Ciudad Villalonga, you would *be* the Archbishop."

"Thanks, son! A thousand thanks! But are you not a little confused? What makes you think that you can make archbishops or even bishops? Her servants can only be chosen by the Mother Church, under the guidance of God."

"God!" Jacinto said. "Where is your God, Old Man? Show Him to me! I want to see Him, now!"

Father Pío got up from where he sat beside Peter's cot, walked over to Jacinto, and tapped him on the chest.

"Here," he said, "in here. And if you would stop shouting and firing off your childish murderous toys, you could hear Him speak. He does, you know. To everyone, in the silence of his heart."

"Good, Father!" Jacinto said. "Good! You hear? I have called you Father. And I am going to go down on my knees like a superstitious peasant, like your cadaver-worshiping Indians, and ask you a thing. Even if your God exists, what good is He? What good at all?"

"My son," Padre Pío began, but Jacinto cut him off.

"What good! When is He ever there when you need Him? Where was He the day the soldiers of Villalonga took my father out of the house after beating him so that he was bloody all over and could not stand? Where was He when they sat my poor little father in a chair and stood my angel from heaven of a mother—she who had no politics at all but was in your fornicating church, praying to your fornicating saints morning, noon, and night—up beside him, both of them without blindfolds, and shot them both? Shot my father who was sitting, through the chest, but my mother, because she was standing, through the lower abdomen, but in both cases badly so that it took them hours to die; and I, who was hidden in the stable under the hay with Guillermo the groom, with his hand which smelled of the dung of horses clamped over my mouth to keep me from crying out, and his whole body which smelled of sweat and tobacco and urine and the sickening stench of fear pressed down on top of me to prevent me from running out to help my parents, could hear them screaming until they could not scream any more and after that moaning until the moans themselves became less than silence. And when I at last broke free of Guillermo and ran to aid them and seeing them there like that, like slaughtered animals in their blood and being unable to stand that either, ran into the house where everything was smashed to bits, and tried to turn on the lights because it was growing dark by then; but there were no lights, because they had cut the wires. So I found my father's flashlight and went to look for my sister Teresa. Where was your monstrous obscenity of a God, Padre, when I found Teresa who was fifteen years old then, found my sister who was beautiful as a flower, pure as the snows on the Sierras, lying there naked in the shreds of the clothes they had ripped off her, in—this, too, Father!—a pool of her own blood on which their filthy semen floated like little white islands? Lying there staring into the beam of the lantern with her mouth and her eyes opened wide trying to cry without tears and to scream without voice?"

"Jesus!" Peter said.

"Do not blaspheme, my son," Padre Pío said. "Go on, Jacinto. I am glad you are telling me this."

"Glad!" Jacinto said. "He is glad! You hear this, Comrade Reporter? He is glad to know how the men, who on Villalonga's orders attend Mass daily, comport themselves when they are out of it! He is proud of his communicants of rapine and murder! You beg the question, Padre! Where was your God when my parents were dying that bad, ugly death? When my sister was praying to Him to let her die also, and He wouldn't even grant her that small mercy?"

"In His heaven, as always," Father Pío said. "Where, very shortly, with that special indulgence granted those who suffer much, your parents and your sister joined Him."

Jacinto raised his two fists to the sky. Threw back his head and howled with laughter. With that kind of laughter that is harder to listen to than crying ever is.

"Now I know!" he said. "I have suspected it a long time! For, if my sister is in heaven, Padre Pío, then heaven is located on the corner of Avenue Bolívar and the Street of the Fourteenth of June! Yes, yes! Your heaven, if it contains my sister, is in La Luna Azul! A whorehouse of a heaven! A heaven of heavenly whores! Oh, they take a man to heaven all right. Better than you do, Padre! Ah yes!"

"Son, you've had it rough, haven't you?" Peter said. "But, since you've told us this much—why not finish it? How'd your sister happen to end up in The Blue Moon?"

Jacinto frowned.

"I think," he said, "it was because after that she did not care. She hated her own body; sought, I think, to debase it. So she did the great act to which we are all born, with anybody. Stable boys, grooms, drunken sailors, Negroes; filthy, stinking Indians smelling of the stench of the dead bodies they keep in their beds. Being lovely still, she caught our Benefactor's eye. Soon she was installed in a palace. Soon she was the mistress of the Head of the State. For a while. For a very little while. Because, since Miguelito is not truly or entirely male, he tires fast. Soon he was—as is his custom—giving her to Luis Sinnombre, that unspeakable beast of all manners of vile practices, while he, Miguel, watched the performance, which is the only way, truly, he can enjoy—"

"So he is a voyeur?" Peter asked.

"I know no French, Comrade," Jacinto said.

"What you have said. One who watches."

"Sí. Among other things. Along with abusing small boys and little girls. And indulging in circuses with Luis and two girls. Or two queers. Or any other combination that excites his capricious nature. He is not the son of Isabela Cienmil for nothing."

"Isabela Cienmil?" Peter said.

"Isabela de los Cienmilamores. Isabela of the Hundred Thousand Loves. She owns The Blue Moon. Or didn't you know that, Comrade?"

"No," Peter said, "I didn't."

"Perhaps she doesn't now. For no one has seen her since she got drunk and made a spectacle of herself at the American Embassy. What a performance! There she was, waving the carving knife under the nose of your so very, very dignified Ambassador who had invited her along with the higher society of Costa Verde, because he, fatuous fool that he is, knew nothing more about her than that the Illustrious Lady was the mother of the Head of the State. And they, the high society who would not have been found dead with that foul-mouthed witch if they hadn't known that to refuse the invitation would be to end up dead indeed, because Miguelito of the French perfumes and delicate practices and ritual murders would be quick to resent the insult, had to sit there and listen to her long dissertation on the art of castration, starting, of course, with the father of Miguel, so that—"

"He could produce no more monsters. I know. I heard that one," Peter said. "But tell me one thing, Comrade Jacinto: If this of the revolution succeeds, what will you do about your sister?"

"Shoot her," Jacinto said.

"My son—" Padre Pío said.

"Shut up, Father! I shall shoot her, Comrade Reporter, with great tenderness, as one shoots an incurably wounded beast. With tenderness, Comrade. With love. Not because of stupid bourgeois prejudices, but to end her sufferings which are unthinkable because there is no pain equal to the pain of self-loathing. So now, Padre Pío, little Father Pious of the death-worshiping Indians, I ask you to bless this pistol with which I will shoot my sister in the back of the neck, ending very quickly and kindly her terrible life. An act of compassion, no? Of Christian charity. With sorrow and pity and tenderness and love. Come on, Father; bless it!"

"No," Padre Pío said.

"Then bless this knife with which I shall rip open the belly of the ugly Alicia once I have used her as her brother's men used my sister!"

"Alicia?" Peter said.

"*His* sister. Alicia Villalonga de Duarte y Marín—who has no more secure right to the name than Miguel has, since old Cienmil doesn't know who her father was either. But his half-sister, anyhow. Whom he adores, despite her ugliness, which is great. Who is now a young widow since Miguelito, having discovered that his brother-in-law was a member of the junta of conservative Army officers plotting to overthrow him, blew up the airplane in which Emilio Duarte was voyaging, killing fifty men and women and three children in order to eliminate Alicia la Fea's adored husband —to the great sorrow of all the chorus girls at the Teatro de la Comedia, all the whores at La Luna Azul, and even of Alicia the Ugly, herself, who, I'm told, loved him. But ugly as she is, I shall mount her. And make him watch it, since he is of this dirty French-named vice you said!"

Juan poked his head through the tent flap.

"All right, Jacinto," he said, "get out. Now—before your ravings attract the notice of the Dictator's Army. They must have heard you even in Ciudad Villalonga, you noisy fool. You heard me! Go!"

Jacinto stood there, looking at his Chief. Then, very slowly, he bent his head and went through the tent flap out into the sunlight, saying no word at all.

"Poor devil," Peter said.

"No," Father Pío said. "I have great hopes for Jacinto now. Do you not see, my son, that what he has said is a kind of confession? That his pain and his anguish are acceptable sacrifices in the eyes of God? I will save him yet—the day I teach him not to hate. You see that I am already gaining ground with him? Today he spoke sincerely, and from the heart—"

"How is your patient, Padre?" Juan broke in.

"Very well. Tomorrow he will be entirely well, fit for all tasks."

Juan smiled. "Have you performed another miracle, Padre? If so, you must be punished. You must know that miracles are against our Socialist concepts—"

"Do not speak of miracles, son," Padre Pío said. "I am not so presumptuous. I know only that I gave him medicine made from the roots of a certain plant the Indios told me about— administered, of course, with prayer. But el Señor Reynolds will be up, and entirely well, tomorrow. You may call it a triumph of Socialist medicine if you like, since it was first proved in your camp. Or, if you prefer, you may call it a miracle of the good God. As what is not, son? Even that we go on walking, breathing air. Or that the sun goes on rising in the mornings, and setting itself at night. Life is a miracle, son. So is love. Tenderness. Compassion. The condition of being human. *Vaya!* You have had your sermon for today!"

"And I go," Juan said, "lest you reduce me to counting glass beads, mumbling nonsense, and burning candles before silly, simpering images of painted plaster. You are in good hands, Comrade Reynolds. Tomorrow I shall look in upon you again."

"All right," Peter said. "But you won't have to. I'll be up. You heard what the good Father said. And I believe him."

"Oh, so do I; so do I," Juan said.

"Son," Father Pío spoke. "I have a thing to say."

"Then say it, Father," Peter said.

"You are Catholic, are you not?" the old priest said.

"I was," Peter said.

"But now you are not?" Father Pío said.

"Now I am nothing. Now I am dirt. No, less than dirt. Garbage."

Father Pío laughed aloud. His laughter was young. Like the roaring of young bulls as they enter the arena.

"Why do you laugh?" Peter said.

"At the nonsense you talk, son! You think that God ever lets go of a man?"

"Padre—I have no skill at talking theology. I only know that too many have died who could have been saved. That too many brave, fine, valuable lives have been snuffed out. And by the bad, the worthless. That there is too much hunger, too much misery, too much sickness, too much pain. I was brought up in the Church, so I know the answers. All the answers. Only they don't satisfy me. Not any more."

"What a presumptuous one! He wants a private explanation from God!"

"No, Father. Because I wouldn't believe Him, either. He's cheated me too many times now. Father, pardon me, but couldn't we just skip this discussion? I am ill, and my head labors badly. It always does, even when I am well."

"Of course," Father Pío said. "It is skipped. No more theology. Tell me, son, are you going to marry Miss Lovell?"

Peter stared at him.

Father Pío smiled.

"No miracles. Not even one. You raved. On the basis of what you said, I could give you absolution, because you hate your sins. Of course, much of the time you were talking English, which I do not understand. But the things you said in Spanish were enough to convince me of your repentance. Now you must tell me consciously that you mean to give it up. Then I will absolve you. I'll make you say two hundred Pater Nosters and five hundred Ave Marias; but nothing more. If you will remove the sin by marrying her, I shall be glad to officiate when we return to the capital—"

"Padre," Peter said, "I can't."

"Why can't you, son?"

"I told you I was brought up in the Church. That part stuck. To me, marriage is just once, and for life."

"I don't understand you son. Not at all."

"I do not wish to be Judith Lovell's fifth husband. Not while the other four are still alive."

"I see," Padre Pío said. "Now I understand. She is a star of the cinema, no?"

"She was; yes," Peter said.

"And not of our Faith?"

"And not of *your* Faith," Peter said.

"How stubborn you are, son! What you must do is very simple. You must leave her."

Peter turned his head away from the old priest. Looked out through the tent flap. The sun was very bright.

"Simple," he said. "Very simple—oh, very simple. Like falling off a log."

"What did you say, son?"

"That nothing is simple. Or everything is. I wouldn't know."

"All right. Your mind wanders. Sleep now, my son—while God and I watch over you."

"You watch over me, Padre. I trust *you*," Peter said.

The next morning he was still dog-sick but he got up anyhow. He wasn't going to let Padre Pío down. He didn't know why, but he couldn't.

"Can't screw up your miracle," he said in English, "you sweet, simple-minded old coot, you . . ."

"What do you say, son?" Padre Pío said.

"That I encounter myself great, fine, enormous," Peter said.

"You don't look it," Father Pío said. "You look like the bad death, son."

"No, of truth I am fine. Come, let us look for Juan. I have a thing to say to him."

"This of the ransom?" Padre Pío said. "He won't take it, Pedro my son."

"Why not?" Peter said.

"Because in his politics, Juan is very pure. They have replaced the religion he thinks he has lost but has not, truly. Neither he nor Jacinto, who is a little mad and hence will become a very great criminal, or a saint. I worry more about Jacinto. With Juan I shall have time."

They came out of the tent together, and the sunlight was

a bundle of golden arrows piercing Peter's eyes. Fire stabbed into his brain under his skull. He reeled a little.

"Son—" Padre Pío said.

Peter straightened up.

"Come on, little Father. Let's go save sinners!" he said.

When they started across the camp under the trees, they saw the Indians. They were coming down from the top of the Sierras in a long double line, hundreds of them. They wore serapes over the ordinary baggy pants and shirts of peons. They had felt hats with big, floppy brims on their heads. Some of the men had a hole punched in the top of their hats with a condor feather stuck into it. They also wore bracelets and necklaces of hammered silver. When they were close enough, Peter could see that the workmanship was very fine.

"Excuse me, son," Padre Pío said, "but now I must attend to my children. They have come a long way—from Xilchimocha, likely—so that I can bless their dead."

"Who are they, Father?" Peter said. "What tribe?"

"I do not know truly. From their features, I should say they are Chibchas, come over the Sierras from Colombia many years ago. Their language is similar to that of the Chibchas, though it has many Toltec words; and others that may be Incan or Mayan, since those words are lost. They call themselves Tluscola, which means only The Men. Or the Real Men. Go back to your tent. Or join Juan. This will take time."

And now, suddenly, Peter saw what the Tluscolas had with them. Saw those straw-wrapped figures in the throne-like chairs. Sitting there upright while four young Tluscola braves bore each chair aloft on long white birch poles set on leather cushions to save their shoulders over all the hundreds of kilometers they must have walked, climbing over the peaks of the Sierras, wading snowdrifts, winding through the passes with their sacred burdens.

And now the wind came down from the peaks, cold and sharp and with a sting of snowflakes in it, light and powdery and dry; but that didn't help that smell. He had smelled it first in Korea, lying in that cave with five of his company dead around him and the maggots moving in the great rent in his shoulder, eating his own hideously stinking flesh, which was why he still had his left arm and why it was only a little stiff in bad weather, because those fat white eaters of putrefaction had left the wound so clean that it healed almost perfectly, leaving only the enormous silver ridge of the scar. He had smelled it again in Hungary, his first big story, and after that in Algiers; and now and again in a hundred places where the thrust and probe of a relentless ideology ran hard up against the stubborn resistance of another that liked to call itself free. He had smelled that smell in Argentina, in Santo Domingo, in Guatemala, in Venezuela, in Colombia—all over Latin America, where fat, porcine little generals bought what they called order with the people's blood. And were maybe the lesser of the two evils, since what it took to strike a balance between thunder on the right and lightning on the left doesn't even exist in the Spanish-speaking world.

But he had never got used to it. It wasn't a thing you got used to: that sweet, sick, utterly vile odor of rotting human flesh. Smelling it now, with the fever still in him, his stomach turned over. He bent his head and vomited, noisily, terribly. Afterwards, he put his back up against a tree, and stayed there, like that, until he saw, five meters to his left, Jacinto lying on his belly, sighting a tripod-mounted Czech copy of a Hotchkiss 9-mm. air-cooled light machine gun, the kind that had the almost-semicircular shell clip mounted on top of the magazine, toward the Indians. Then he moved, crossing the distance that separated him and Jacinto in five long strides, got there, his right foot swinging back, his weight pivoted on his left, bringing that right foot forward, clad in and protected by his stout Alpine boots, to crash against the barrel of the gun, sending it over and to one side so that the short, ripping snarl of the burst Jacinto got off, either deliberately, or because his finger was still on the trigger when

Peter kicked, cut a pine sapling in two and sent it crashing down.

Jacinto's expression didn't change. He simply put his hand to his belt and came out with his Commando knife, with which he could have shaved if beards hadn't become the latest ideological symbol. Then he kicked free of the overturned gun and got up without haste, looking at Peter with those flat yellow eyes without anger in them or hate or anything at all but that ice-cold mindless glare of the great predators to whom killing is neither an emotion nor a conditioned reflex but an instinct, requiring nothing more than opportunity.

Peter stood there in a great blaze of sunlight, his arms down to his sides, unmoving, watching Jacinto's arm going back in that smooth underhand swing, the light glinting on the blade and the smell of burned cordite in his nostrils now, the vile green taste of nausea in his throat, noting all his own sensations with detachment and curiosity, just as though he were going to be around to analyze them later, as if they mattered, which they didn't, any more than the act of dying did to him then, considering what his life was like now, and was going to be.

Father Pío's voice, when it spoke, wasn't even loud. It was, in fact, curiously gentle.

"Stop it, Jacinto," he said.

Jacinto looked at his knife. Then he put it back into the sheath. Bent and picked up the machine gun, put it right side up. Took an oily rag out of the toolbox beside it and began to wipe the dirt off the barrel, digging it out of the slots of the barrel with a part of the rag.

"Better dismantle it," Peter said. "It's surely got dirt in the magazine. Next time you fire it, it'll jam, or blow up."

Jacinto nodded. Then he dropped to his haunches and began to take the gun apart, laying each piece out on a piece of oilskin, very, very carefully.

"Go back to your tent, son," Father Pío said. "It has passed. He will not trouble you again."

But before Peter could move, Juan was there.

"Jacinto," he said.

"Yes, Chief?" Jacinto said.

"You were going to kill the Indians, no?"

"Sí, Jefe," Jacinto said.

"Why?" Juan said.

"Why not?" Jacinto said. "They love death. Why not give them what they love?"

"And Peter? Does he also love death?"

"Yes. When I came to kill him, he did not even lift a hand. He waited, and was glad."

"Jacinto—" Juan said.

"Yes, Juan?"

"You are not to kill, understand? Only those I tell you. Our enemies. The enemies of the people. Do you comprehend, Camarada?"

"Yes, Juanito. I understand."

"Look, Comrade Reynolds," Juan said, "there is no time to discuss this of your proposal to ransom Padre Pío. Because now we must break camp and move with great haste."

"Why?" Peter said.

"Because of the Indians. If they have not been seen by the airplanes of Villalonga—the ones with which the great democratic country of the United States so kindly supplied him—it is truly one of Padre Pío's miracles. Hundreds of them heading straight to this place. It is like a great arrow pointing, you know. This is the third time we've had to move because of them."

"How do they know where he is?" Peter said.

Juan frowned.

"I do not know," he said.

"They smell him," Jacinto said. "He smells as they do— of death. Stinking Indians! Hauling their dead across the mountains so Tío Pío can bless them, then hauling them all the way back home again. And, afterwards, he will have to go to Xilchimocha to make sure they have actually buried them instead of sleeping with them like the necrophiliacs

they are! Ha! Perhaps he is, too! Ah ha, Uncle Pío! Do you
like a little piece of dead tail from time to time?"

"Shut up, animal!" Juan said. "He makes a bad joke, Comrade Reporter. The Tluscola do not use the dead sexually,
as this beast knows very well. That would be a heinous
blasphemy to them, which they would punish by the most
cruel death they could devise. But come, then, you are well
enough to ride, are you not—after Father Pío's latest
miracle?"

"Yes," Peter said.

"Then I will ride with you, as the Indios have brought
Father Pío a horse as a gift to recompense him for his mumbling Latin and sprinkling water over their maggoty
corpses. I think they mean for him to use it to escape. So I
will forestall him. I will borrow it. Then you and I will ride
out to find a new campsite—as inaccessible as possible."

"You want *me* to go with you?" Peter said.

"Yes. So that you can tell me about your interview with
Fidel in las Sierras Madres—before he came to power. I can
learn much from that," Juan said.

"You can. But you won't. At least not the essential," Peter
said.

"And that is?"

"To call the whole thing off." Peter said.

3.

When they found that place, it looked very fine, a wood of
fir and balsam and pine growing on one of the shoulders of
the mountain with a vertical precipice that dropped five
hundred meters straight down on one side of it, of shale rock
that even a fly couldn't have scaled, let alone a man, with

no way into the woods except up a tongue of ancient solidified lava from the days when the whole Sierra had been as active as Zopocomapetl was now, over which an army could have marched single file without leaving tracks, and no way out of it, so far as Peter could see, at all. On the other side of the woods opposite the precipice, the peak of the mountain went straight up at an angle that—if it wasn't ninety—was at least eighty-five degrees.

"Like it?" Juan said.

"No," Peter said.

"Why not?"

"Because this is a campsite for heroes, and I am a coward." Juan smiled.

"A rare sort of coward, Comrade," he said. "But, seriously, what is wrong with it?"

"As a base from which to attack, nothing. As a natural fortress, formidable. Give me a machine gun and enough ammunition and the food to last a year, and I personally could eliminate Villalonga's Army."

"So?" Juan said.

"I have already said it. Think about it," Peter said.

"I have thought. And it is perfect, Comrade Reporter! First they have to find us, and those trees make wonderful cover. Say they have found us. They have to make a frontal attack up a tongue of volcanic rock so narrow that only two men can walk abreast. What a slaughter! Why—"

"Juanito—" Peter said.

"What?" Juan said, frowning.

"They don't have to attack. They merely have to camp down there at the foot of that lava tongue, with jeeps bringing them food, hot food, every day, with the smell of it blowing up here to where you starve. Out of range of your knee mortars and your light machine guns. Then, when they have got tired of waiting, they will hitch a couple of those old French Seventy-fives from the first world war, which still shoot pretty good, son, behind their jeeps, bring them up to that nice flat little plateau down there at the foot of the lava tongue and start lobbing shrapnel in here. And incendiaries. And wait down there at the foot of that one-way street you're so proud of for you and yours to come out of the woods which will be burning by then. Or stay in them and roast. Or throw yourselves over that precipice. Because your choices will be reduced to that, Comrade—various highly unpleasant ways to die."

Juan sat there on the horse, looking at Peter.

"Of course I forgot something," Peter said.

"What have you forgot?"

"That Khrushchev and Castro will, of course, airlift troops and ammunition and food to you. That solves your problem of logistics. And our President, of course, will hide under his desk in the White House, and let them do it. He wouldn't dream of sending the Atlantic Fleet, or a few jet fighters, or even the Marines to interfere, now would he?"

Juan used the sharp, explosive Spanish word *"Mierda!"* which means fecal matter in English, but you can't translate it with English. You have to use Anglo-Saxon.

"Right," Peter said, "and you've had it, chum. You've been buried in it, up to the eyes."

Juan went on looking at those woods.

"Have you seen anything better?" he said.

"No," Peter said. "And this will do for a hiding place for a few days. Maybe even a week. But if they even start getting close, you'd better move on."

They hauled the horses' heads around, and started back down again.

"About Padre Pío . . ."

"No," Juan said.

"Look, Juan!" Peter said. "With the money my paper's paying, you could *buy* Ciudad Villalongal Then you wouldn't have to—"

"No," Juan said again.

"And if I try to sneak him out of the camp one fine dark night?"

"I should let Jacinto handle it. That's his department."

"I see. You pass the buck. You delegate murder to other hands."

"Something like that," Juan said. "But seriously, Comrade, do you think even an ant could get out of our camp if I gave orders for him not to?"

"You've got something there. Your sentries are pretty nervous types. Still, I wish you'd let me bail Padre Pío out. He's too old to—"

"No," Juan said again.

"Why not?" Peter said.

"Because only he can deliver the Indians to us. They are essential. Without them we shall never prevail against the Spanish upper class, and the middle class, which is Mestizo. How can one have a Dictatorship of the Proletariat without the proletariat? Or a People's Democracy without the people?"

"Will you let them go on keeping Grandpa's corpus delicti in the living room?"

"*Hombre*, I will go them one better! I will teach them taxidermy and supply them with artificial glass eyes. I will teach them how to achieve a high gloss on Abuelito's mangy hide; how to stuff him with pleasant-smelling straw, perfume his gray plaits, coat the condor feather in his hair with a long-lasting insecticide, how even to stand him up in the foyer in a lifelike pose, with his arms extended so that he may be useful as a hatrack, say. Why, I'll even . . ."

It was then that they heard the plane.

They were below the forest by then, going down a well-marked trail. On both sides of that trail the slopes fell away in a long gentle curve of sheet rock, and old ash rotting now into soil. They could have gone down those slopes easily enough, except there was no reason to go down them since their nakedness, their total absence of cover, was now, under the circumstances in which they found themselves, not merely indecent but obscene.

For that bellow blasting the sky apart wasn't any eighty-five horsepower Lycoming in a Cub. That was a double-row eighteen-hundred-horsepower Pratt and Whitney, close-cowled into the nose of a cranked-wing Vought Corsair.

Looking up, Peter could see the red and yellow markings with the thin purple cross like the letter X that Miguel Villalonga had copied with slavish lack of imagination, only reversing the order of the colors, from the Army of the Air of Spain.

"Blood, pus, and permanganate," he said. Then, seeing Juan digging his heels into the big-chested, finely built roan the Indians had brought as a gift for Padre Pío, he shouted:

"For God's sake, don't run!"

But he was too late because the big roan was already off and away, and he, sawing at the bit of his shaggy mountain pony, trying to hold him, saw those curious cranked, reverse gull wings which were the distinguishing feature of the World War Two-vintage fighter—the last propeller-driven pursuit in active service, having lasted through Korea before being retired, where, as now, it had proved itself on ground-support missions the jets were just too fast to manage —heel over in a vertical bank; peeling off, screaming down, that beautiful blue-painted image of sudden death, rocking level now, pulling up five kilometers behind them, but coming on, the prop a mist-silver disk scribed about with a perfect circle of orange; and he, that red-hot pilot, that authentic blue-flame boy, one of the twenty-five young Costa Verdian aristocrats, sons of landowners, manufacturers, coffee, sugar, and oil fortunes, trained at Keeler Field, Mississippi, at San Antonio, Texas, and in California, as a sort of technical lend lease to do effortlessly, perfectly, what he was doing now.

His run was straight out of the textbook. He cranked down full flaps, even lowered his landing gear to slow him down enough, and floated in, looking for all the world like a vulture headed for carrion; except that this particular group of four-footed and two-legged carrion was momentarily still alive.

Then, looking up and back, Peter saw the leading edge of the Corsair's wing start its acetylene blowtorch splutter in four separate and distinct places, the white line of tracers arching out, and the fifty-caliber Browning slugs throwing up a column of dirt and rock that came quick-stepping down the road behind him like a platoon of dancing, idiotic ghosts. And he, Peter, diving out of the saddle head-first into a shallow ditch beside the trail, the breath going out of him and night coming down to lift only when he heard his pony scream, high and shrill like a woman in pain.

And, lifting his gaze, seeing the shaggy beast with its head down now, vomiting blood, and the red tide pouring out of it through a line of holes stitched along all its flank, watching that, unable to see Juan at all, hearing the rustling back washing wall of air from the prop going over and past and a shower of shells from the ejector chutes bounding and glittering on the road; and the plane banking, climbing, tucking its wheels up into the wing boots again, then screaming down in a shallow dive, but pulling up short, far short of the target, which he still couldn't see because he was too far down off the trail, but seeing what he could see easily enough, that the pull-up hadn't been short after all, because that fat, finned bomb continued the trajectory the plane had started it on, whistling down in a long, only slightly curving arc to end time, to stop the world.

He saw it. Saw that little black rag doll rise with both arms and the one leg it had left extended, flying now, borne up on the blast, hanging in midair in apparent defiance of gravity for a segment of time that could not have been more than the barest measurable fraction of a second, but which Peter's own pain, shock, horror extended unbearably until his arrested breath, life, heartbeat started once more and renewed perception let that nothing blasted out of the middle of existence become something, become Juan's body arching downward, falling now, whistling earthward amid the thick showering shale rock amid the pieces of the horse.

And he, Peter, getting up, forgetting the plane that was already nothing but a blue crooked cross silhouetted against the dark plume of Zopocomapetl, and stumbling, falling, getting up again until he reached the place where Juan lay—miraculously but not mercifully alive, the life draining out of him through that shredded mass of red rags and splintered bone where his right leg ended just below the knee. And Peter bending, whipping off his belt, looping it around Juan's thigh, tightening it in ferocious jerks until the red tide slowed. Then, afterward, tearing off his own shirt and wrapping it around the stump in a clumsy bandage. And standing there, looking at Juan, but not thinking because there was nothing to think about now; only things to be done.

He went back to where his pony lay dead in the road and got his canteen from the saddlebag. He wasted five minutes searching for Juan's amid the chopped, splattered meat and the pink, slimy sausage rolls of horse guts. Then he gave it up. He lifted Juan onto his back by the arms and started down that trail.

In the first kilometer, he didn't fall even once. But in the second he fell three times. In the third, five. By the fifth, he was averaging a hundred meters between falls. In the middle of the sixth kilometer, he knew he wasn't going to be able to get up again, so he eased Juan off his back and tried to force some water between his lips which were swollen and black and oozing blood at the corners. He couldn't. So he took a drink himself, and lay there.

When the first shadow passed over his head he thought it was the plane come back again. But it hadn't made any noise so he looked up and saw that it was a forked-tail kite. Then another one passed over, and another and another until the air was black with them, circling. He moved his arms in a waving motion and all the kites screamed and lifted. But they didn't go away. They only circled higher. Then a bigger shadow drifted across the road and dropped the trailing edge of its wings to an almost vertical position, stopping itself dead in midair. Its red, scaly feet came out of its dark belly and spread, gripping a rock. Then it sat there, looking at him, its eyes black and patient in the midst of its bluish-red, bald, scaly head.

Peter tried waving his hand at it, but it paid no attention. He clawed his fingers into the surface of the road for loose rocks, threw them one by one at the buzzard. He was too weak. They all fell short. The buzzard sat there looking at him. The kites circled lower now, screaming.

He saw the others coming in, but he was too tired and too sick to count them. The rocks on both sides of the road were covered with them now. When the last one came in, he was sure it was a plane, it was so much bigger than the others. But then he saw that red, turkey-cock comb on the top of its head, and knew it was a condor. The others made room for it. It sat in their midst, head and shoulders taller than the rest.

He lay there looking at them. From time to time he sipped the water in the canteen. He was beginning to feel a little better, enough, maybe, to make another five meters before he'd fall again. Then he remembered that Juan was probably wearing his sidearm. He groped for it, found it, dragged it out of the holster. He held it in his two hands, pointed at the condor. Squeezed. But the safety catch was on. He flipped it off, squeezed the trigger again. The Mauser-type automatic bucked and roared. The condor fell over in a sodden heap. The buzzards rose heavily, clumsily, found an updraft, soared.

Five minutes later, Jacinto and a scouting party were there.

Jacinto looked at Juan. He didn't say anything. He simply lifted his machine pistol toward where the kites and buzzards circled. He got five of them before it barked empty.

One of the others was working on Juan's leg. He seemed to know what he was doing, so Peter looked away toward Jacinto.

"How—" he said.

"Your shot, Comrade Reporter. Of course we heard that profanity of an airplane. We even heard it machine-gunning the road. When it dropped the bomb, we knew it had you. But we came anyhow. When you fired at the condor and the other carrion birds flew up, you pinpointed this place for us."

He turned to the other one who was working on Juan.

"Is he going to die, Pepe?" he said.

"Yes," Pepe said. "He has lost too much blood. If the Yanqui hadn't applied the tourniquet, he would be dead by now."

"Soon?" Jacinto said.

"How do I know?" Pepe said. "He might die in five minutes, or in five hours. I cannot tell. But it would be better if he died now, without regaining consciousness; or else we shall have to use up all our morphine on him. Because, Comrade Second Chief, that vileness of a leg is going to hurt with a vileness unspeakable, and if the pilot of that plane has told them to scout in this area, his screams well might give us away."

"You think it advisable to shoot him, then?" Jacinto said.

"Jacinto, for the love of God!" Peter said.

"God does not exist, Comrade Reporter," Jacinto said. "Do not speak idiocies; it distracts my attention. And now, I must think."

Peter lay there, looking at those yellow eyes. They were withdrawn and rapt. Then they cleared.

"We will take him to the camp. Perhaps he has orders to give us. And, in any case, if he screams too much, we can always shoot him there."

Peter let out his breath, slowly.

Jacinto looked at him. Then he roared with laughter. It sounded like the howl of a timber wolf.

"You see?" he said to the others. "He still has fever! Now will you cease to speak of the miracles of the ugly little Vasco? Or would you say the Yankee has no faith?"

"He is a heretic. A Protestant," Pepe said.

"No, he is Catholic," Jacinto said. "I heard him say so to Uncle Pío."

"Look, Jacinto," Pepe said. "With this of the revolution, of accord. There have been many abuses which we can only remedy by killing the abusers. And I am a Communist. I do not believe in God—not any longer. But I have seen the little Basque Father do too many things for which there are no reasonable explanations. So, as practical men, why take chances? Look at the vile vileness of the luck we have been having lately. So, Comrade Chief, may I respectfully suggest that you cease to fornicate with their fornicating God?"

"And I," Jacinto said, "may I suggest, with no respect at all, that you cease to gamble upon the fact that you are the only one among us who has any knowledge of medicine? Considering the equally important fact that you were suspended in all your examinations at the Medical School, your domination of medical science is insufficient to make me think overlong about whether or not I should shoot you, Comrade Doctor! Now pick up poor Juan and march!"

Nobody bothered to pick Peter up. But with a shot of rum in him from the canteen of the young third officer called Federico, who made sure Jacinto was not looking when he offered it, Peter found that he could walk. Slowly, stumbling along, but upright. By the time they got back to camp, he was bone-weary and aching all over. But Father Pío was right; the fever was gone.

And now the three of them—José, called Pepe as all Josés are called in Spanish by their friends for some long forgotten reason, Father Pío, and Peter—watched over Juan. Pepe was a better doctor, or at least a better surgeon, than Jacinto gave him credit for. He boiled his instruments, cut away the shredded flesh, sawed off the splintered bone, leaving a neat flap of skin which he sewed over Juan's knee to make a stump. He dusted the wound with sulfa, shot a million units of penicillin into Juan's veins. Stood back, watching. Said:

"He is in shock. What he needs is a transfusion. But we have no plasma."

"Blood," Peter said, sitting there with the sweat pouring out of him from having watched it. "Take mine."

"Or mine," Father Pío said.

"No," Pepe said.

"Why not?" Peter said.

"I do not know his blood type. Nor yours. Nor Uncle

Pío's. Nor mine. You know what happens when you give the wrong type blood?"

"Yes," Peter said. "It kills the patient. But, since he is going to die anyhow, why not gamble upon it?"

"I prefer him to die. I do not wish to kill him," Pepe said.

"Son," Padre Pío said, "it seems to me that you are wrong. If you make no effort to save him, the guilt is in part yours. If you do make the effort, and he dies, then clearly his death is the will of God . . ."

"God does not exist," Pepe parroted. "*Mierda!* Do not tangle me in your Jesuit sophistries, Padre! I have done what I could. But if he dies in convulsions as the result of a transfusion, Jacinto will shoot me, surely. Jacinto loves him much."

"I don't think Jacinto loves anybody," Peter said.

"Oh yes, he does," Pepe said. "You saw that back there on the trail he gave up the pleasure of shooting him? And if you knew how Jacinto enjoys shooting people! It is his greatest delight——"

"I gathered as much," Peter said.

"Son—the transfusion," Padre Pío said.

"No. I am sorry, Padre; but I am not that much of an altruist. I want to live," Pepe said.

They sat there, watching Juan. He was very quiet. Father Pío put out his right hand and bathed Juan's forehead. Peter saw that round, deep sunken bluish scar in the middle of his right hand.

"This," he said to the old priest. "How did it occur, Father? Or is it that you bear the stigmata of Our Lord?"

Father Pío laughed softly.

"I am not worthy of such an honor," he said. "No, son, a bullet made that. In Spain, during the Civil War. I was blessing the firing squad who shot me."

Peter looked at him.

"You were blessing the Red execution platoon who—"

"Not the Reds. The others. But apart from that minor detail, yes. I was blessing the soldiers who were trying to kill me."

Pepe stared at him.

"You mean to say, Uncle Pío, that it was the Fascists who shot you? You, a priest?"

"But a Basque priest," Father Pío said. "That made a difference."

"How?" Pepe said.

"Because in Vasconia we did not spend our time moaning over the terrible crimes of the Reds—and they *were* terrible, son; more terrible than you imagine—we simply asked ourselves what it was the Church had done, that Spanish men, unquestionably the most loyal of all her sons, could come to hate her so."

"And what had the Church done?" Peter said.

"Neglected them, followed the age-old, blind policy of siding with the rich, the powerful. Advised them to submit, to be patient, to be humble. To work fourteen hours a day for wages too small to feed their families. For in Vasconia we knew even then what all Catholics have learned since: that social justice *is* the business of the Church. That if we do not insure it, the Reds will use the misery of the poor as the lever to overthrow us."

"Let us not speak of politics," Peter said, "or even of religion, which are subjects of insupportable heaviness. But, speak of your execution, Father. I have seen many men shot as spies, and they do not survive. Twelve men in a firing squad are unlikely to miss. This was another of your miracles, then?"

"Son Pedro," Father Pío said, "I have not the power of miracle-working. If I had, do you think I should permit this slaughter between brothers? Or the traffic in women that goes on in Ciudad Villalonga?"

"Yet," Peter said, "they shot you, and you live."

"Three of them shot me, son. The rest fired over my head. And even those three did it badly. You see, they were from Navarra. Royalists, and the most devout Catholics on earth. It upset them to have to shoot a priest. Even a Red priest, as they called us. Afterwards, I'm told, with the other twenty-four of us they shot for the crime of lending spiritual comfort to those Republican soldiers who wanted it—and there were many such, Son Pepe, despite their exposure to your Marxist nonsense—they got used to it. But I was the first, and it upset them. They were very young, as they were all crying. Even the lieutenant commanding them was crying. When he approached me to give me the shot of mercy, he saw at once that I was not badly hurt. So he whispered, 'Father, can you hear me?' And I said: '*Sí, hijo*.' He said: 'Can you hold out two hours until I can come back?' I had much pain, but I told him I could. So he straightened up and shouted 'No need to waste a shot on this filthy Red! He is already buzzard food!' Then they marched away."

"And?" Pepe said.

"I crawled away from there into another street. A woman found me. A woman whose son had been murdered by the Reds. She took me in. I spent the rest of the war as a woodcutter by day and a priest by night. At the end I escaped over the mountains into France. That's all."

On the cot, Juan stirred, moaned. They all bent over him. But he was still again. They sat there, watching him. An hour later he woke up and started to scream.

Peter held him while Pepe prepared the needle. Shot the morphine into him. But it didn't take effect. He kept on screaming until Jacinto came into the tent with his pistol in his hand.

Father Pío got up, stood between Jacinto and the cot. "No, son!"

Jacinto slammed him to the floor with the flat side of the pistol.

Pepe edged toward the door.

Peter came upright then, slowly and carefully and quietly. "Jacinto—"

"*Mierda?* Screw you, Gringo!"

"Your mother," Peter said. Spanish profanity is an art. You don't have to be explicit. You simply pick out your opponent's closest female relative. He'll know what you mean. As Jacinto did now.

He whirled upon Peter, those yellow eyes luminous as sparks. Then, slowly, he stopped. Began to laugh.

"You want to provoke me, Comrade? Then try something else. I am past all the notions I was born to—even that one. A woman is only an animal for breeding. Any woman— even my mother. So go on, curse me! Speak of it. This you will do in the bad milk of that. This was done by my mother, by my grandmother, by my great-grandmother. My father was perverted, my grandfather the Queen of the Fairies. Go on! Speak of it!"

"No," Peter said.

"Why not?"

"I do not waste breath. We have too little. I say only this: If you so much as point your Czechoslovakian toy toward Juan, I shall take it away from you and break your teeth out with it. By the long route. By shoving it up you till it protrudes. Is this entirely clear?"

"*Vaya!*" Jacinto said. Then his mood changed. "Look, Comrade Reporter, I have no wish to shoot Juan. We have been friends since we were little boys. It would pain me much to hurt him. But I am commander now, and the whole band cannot be sacrificed for one man!"

"Wait," Peter said. "Pepe!"

"Yes, Comrade?"

"Bind up his mouth. With gauze. Tape it shut. It will not make him suffer more; and it will keep our valiant Chief from having to shoot him."

"That is intelligent," Jacinto said. "Do it, Pepe. I order you to do it." Then he turned and marched out.

Peter helped the old priest up from the ground. He was bleeding from a cut above his right eye. Pepe finished gagging Juan, got up, came over and attended to that, too. Cleaned the blood and dirt out of it. Dusted it with sulfa.

"He is a savage, Jacinto!" Pepe said.

"He has suffered much, son," Father Pío said.

Peter lifted his hand suddenly. Pepe and the old priest stopped talking. Stared at him.

"Juan," Peter said. "Look at Juan!"

Juan's eyes were wide open. They moved slowly. He was

looking into their faces. His eyes focused properly. They were clear.

"Juan," Peter said, "can you hear me?"

Juan nodded his head. Very slowly. With immense effort.

"You want me to take the gag from your mouth?" Peter said.

Juan nodded. More slowly now.

"And you will not scream?"

The movement of Juan's head was barely perceptible.

"Take it off, Pepe," Peter said.

Pepe hesitated.

"Take it off!" Peter said.

Pepe removed the pad of gauze he had taped over Juan's mouth.

"Thanks," Juan said. The word was hushed, death-dry, and rattling. "Peter—" Juan said.

"Sí, Juanito?" Peter said.

"You—it was you who brought me in, no?"

"No," Peter said. "Pepe and Jacinto and the rest found us."

"After you had made five kilometers with him on your back," Pepe said. "Perhaps I retrogress to bourgeois morality, but I prefer truth. He saved you, Juanito. The Comrade Gringo saved you. And now I wonder—"

"What?" Juan said.

"If they will work, our revolution, our new Socialist state. If they ever can. Do we not need, maybe, even this ancient monkey of a Basque, and his superstitious mumbo-jumbo? When a man is alone and surrounded on his last hill, what then, Juanito? You are near death. And the dying speak truly. Tell me, Comrade, whether—"

"No," Peter said. "He is too weak. Do not make him talk."

"Then you, Comrade," Pepe said; "you who have traveled much, and lived in many lands. Are we right? Or do we merely replace one evil with another?"

"Do not ask me these things," Peter said, still watching Juan. "I am not wise enough to answer. Ask Father Pío. That's his department."

"No," Pepe said. "He is of a prejudiced point of view."

"You think I'm not?" Peter said.

"No. It seems to me that you generally speak justly. Juanito, does our talking disturb you?"

Juan shook his head.

"Water," he said. "I have thirst. Give me water. Then talk."

Father Pío held the canteen to his mouth. He drank painfully. Moved his head aside.

"Talk," he said.

"We had better not," Peter said; "perhaps——"

"Talk!" Juan said. "I want to hear——to know——"

"And I," Jacinto said, coming into the hut. "Yes, Comrade Reporter, talk! Let us determine whether we already have a Titoist movement of deviationists upon our hands."

Saying that, his voice had changed. And now it came to Peter why. He was consciously trying to talk like the Chief of a Communist guerrilla band. But using the ponderous and meaningless shibboleths of Marxists' jargon which had been imposed upon him from without—during his training in Cuba, probably—and which had penetrated neither his mind nor his heart, Jacinto was merely ridiculous. No—pitiful.

"Which you will then settle by shooting everybody?" Peter said.

"No, not everybody," Jacinto said, "just the ones with the stink of corruption in them, like our Pepe here. But do not let me interrupt you, Comrades. This is a democracy, no? And free speech is permitted, is it not? At least while the speaker lives . . ."

Pepe's head came up.

"Look, Jacinto," he said, "your jokes are not diverting. Nor your half-hidden threats. It seems to me that your mania for killing people will one day cause your own death. And I will speak. I will say what I think. Principally I think that you are mad and a danger to our cause!'

Jacinto laid his machine pistol down on the ground at the foot of Juan's cot. Took out his Beretta automatic and put it beside the burp gun and his knife.

"Now," he said, smiling out of his flat yellow eyes rather than with his mouth, "I am unarmed. I can kill no one. Speak."

"All right," Pepe said. "Comrade Reporter, do you think we shall prevail?"

"Yes," Peter said.

"And afterwards, what?" Pepe said.

"Afterwards, nothing," Peter said.

"You mean we will not end the abuses?"

"I mean you will substitute others."

"Why?" Pepe said.

"Because you are not Anglo-Saxons. Or Danes. Or Swedes."

"You mean we're no good?" Jacinto said.

"I mean you're Latinos," Peter said.

"And hence no good?" Jacinto said.

"No," Peter said, "I do not mean that. You have virtues enough, God knows. Let us say you are not sufficiently slow of thought or cold of blood. Which is why you are of such rare political ineptitude."

"*Ha!*" Jacinto said.

Peter looked at him.

"Have you ever heard of any country where a man of your race has set foot that has not had twenty-five revolutions and fifty dictators by now?"

"I will accept that," Pepe said. "Will you accept our contention that these are the things that *we* will remedy?"

"No," Peter said.

"Why not?" Jacinto said.

"Because," Peter said, "I was in Russia. And in Hungary. And in Cuba."

"You, Comrade Reporter," Jacinto said, "are the classic reactionary."

"Will you shut up, Jacinto?" Pepe said. "Look, Comrade, according to the Party theoreticians, the things we do now: the shooting of deviationists—"

"The torture of prisoners. Brainwashing. The extermination of thousands, even millions when it seems necessary . . ."

"Lies!" Jacinto said.

"I was there," Peter said; "I saw."

"Let me finish," Pepe said. "Let me present the orthodox Leninistic point of view—about which, frankly, Comrade Yanqui, I have my reservations. But, for argument's sake, let me present it. Those things, Comrade Reporter, great as they seem to you and me because of our bourgeois intellectual background, are, in the scale of history, very small. And temporary measures only, until true peoples' democracies can be established everywhere. I confess this theory does not sit well on my overly sensitive stomach. Do you, my friend, believe that good can come out of evil? Even great good out of very little evil? Do you, Comrade?"

Peter grinned at him.

"Do you believe that a woman can be only a little pregnant?" he said. "Or that a *chica* can lose only a little of her virginity? Or, if Jacinto of the Yellow Eyes were to shoot me, as he is clearly desirous of doing, that I should be only a little dead?"

"No," Jacinto said, "you would be dead all right. Totally."

"This is a clever statement, son," Father Pío said. "Carry it further."

"It goes no further," Peter said. "And we have tired Juan enough. How goes it, old one?"

"Badly," Juan said. "Jacinto—"

"Sí, Jefe?" Jacinto said.

"He—is to be released. He—and the priest. An order. My last. You have heard me?"

"But Juan!" Jacinto said.

"Order. Padre . . ."

"Yes, son?"

"Come," Juan said.

The old priest got up, went to the side of the cot.

"You," Juan said; and now, suddenly, his voice was strong. "You, Jacinto, and you, Pepe, get out. You, Peter, stay."

"Why?" Peter said.

"Because you are a Christian. Father—"

"Yes, my son?"

"I—" His voice went abruptly out of sound. Peter could

see his lips move, and leaned close. The words came up to him in a fetid stink of fever-laden breath.

"*Ave Maria, llena de gracia, el Señor esta——*"

And he, Peter, saying it, too—in English, because that was the language he'd learned it in, as a child—trying to recapture the miracle and the privilege of innocence, the simple joy of believing in something, anything; and failing, as always; but saying it anyhow, forcing the words out over the barrier of disuse, over the mountains of doubt, the crags of intellectual pride:

"—is with Thee. Blessed art Thou among women."

And Father Pío, taking it up:

"*Bendita sea el fruta de tu vientre——*"

"Jesus. Holy Mary, Mother of God—"

"*Santa Maria, Madre de Dios,*" Juan whispered.

"Pray for us, sinners—"

"*Reza por nosotros, pecadores——*"

"Now, and at the hour of our deaths, Amen."

"*Ahora y en la hora,*" Juan began. And ended it there; because for him the hour was now, visible, and at hand.

"Padre?" Peter said.

"What a beautiful death!" the old priest said.

4.

They buried Juan in the middle of the campsite, piling rocks on his grave so that no animal would be able to dig him up. Father Pío made a cross of wood, on which he carved Juan's name, his dates—pitifully close together—and the notation, "He Returned to the Faith." But when he had set it up, Jacinto came out of his tent and kicked it over. The old priest set it up again. This time, when Jacinto started toward it, Pepe got in front of him.

"You will not do this again, Jacinto," he said.

"Who will stop me?" Jacinto said.

"I," Pepe said.

"And after you lie beside him, who will stop me?" Jacinto said.

"I," Peter said.

Jacinto stood there, looking at them both.

"And finally, God will stop you," Padre Pío said.

Jacinto's gaze moved, lambent and pale, from face to face to face. Then he turned without saying anything at all, and started back toward his tent.

But, before he got there, they heard the noise of motors, laboring up the trail.

Jacinto turned. What was in his face was very simple and uncomplicated and terrible and sure. It was joy.

"Pepe!" he said. "Go tell Federico to form ranks! Now we have them! Now we will take them from both sides of the trail and—"

"How will you do that?" Peter said. "Since, from the sound of them, they are already past this place, searching for my cadaver and Juan's and those of the horses?"

"Simple! We will attack from both flanks and—"

"Jacinto," Peter said.

"Now what?" Jacinto said.

"Do you not remember the topography of the trail above the camp?"

"I do," Pepe said. "It is as bare as the buttocks of a baby six months old. Additionally, the trail follows the ridge so that we would be visible to them long before we got to the side of the road. We should have to attack uphill under the fire of fifty-caliber BARs which can kill us at a distance that these little toys of ours cannot carry; and tomorrow we would be hanging upside down for the moral edification of the populace in the Plaza of the Liberation."

"Remove your pants!" Jacinto said.

"Remove my pants?" Pepe said. "Why?"

"I wish to see what, if anything, you have in them."

"What I have in them is of both a sufficiency and an excess to make all your female relatives scream in delight and in pain," Pepe said, "but what is more important is what I have in my head. Brains—unscrambled by either hate or suffering, Jacinto. Listen, old one, you are Chief. But I am now Second in Command. And, just as Juan often listened to you, at least in those situations where valor and speed counted more than intelligence, so must you listen to me—as I will listen to Federico when they have killed you, and I become Jefe, and he Second—"

"I am listening," Jacinto said.

"Is it our purpose to display our bravery or to win this war?" Pepe asked.

"There, you have a point," Jacinto said, "still—"

"Still nothing," Peter said. "If you wish to die, cut your throat, and we will bury you beside Juan. For to attack up a slope without cover, against heavier fire than you can answer, unsupported by either aviation or artillery, is suicide, Jacinto."

"How would you know, newsvendor?" Jacinto said.

Peter opened his shirt. The great scar running from his left shoulder to his armpit was ice-white against the sun-blackened darkness of his skin. So were all the other whorls and crescents and rips and tears of shrapnel that covered his chest. He took the shirt off. Slowly he turned his back to Jacinto. The long slope of his shoulders, the trapezoidal V of back muscles, lean and powerful, were teak-colored and clean.

"Do you see anything here, Jacinto?" he said over his shoulder.

"*Madre de Dios!*" Pepe said.

"Blasphemy serves for nothing, son," Padre Pío said.

"But it is not possible!" Pepe said. "No man could take that many wounds and live!"

"As you can see, I did," Peter said. "It is not even very unusual when one has the luck to be caught on the far edge of a shell burst instead of at its center. The record, I think, was held by the writer Hemingway, who took one hundred fifty-four pieces of shrapnel at one time, on the River Piave, in Italy, during the first world war, and survived. Which has no importance now. What does have significance is that I got these mounting an attack up a snow-covered hill against your good friends the Chinese Reds. So this of uphill attacks with insufficient firepower I know, Jacinto. I had the lesson rammed into me in ninety-three separate places—most of them, fortunately, smaller than birdshot. So forget this madness, will you? There where the slopes have the shape of the anatomies of the girls at the Blue Moon and rather less natural foliage, it cannot be done."

"All right," Jacinto said. "I am prepared to be reasonable. And to accept the advice of the heroic Comrade Gringo. What do you think should be done, Comrade?"

"I think," Peter said, "that we should get the hell out of here."

Jacinto looked at him through those flat yellow eyes. A long time. A very long time. Then he sighed.

"So be it; we will retreat," he said.

They went down from the camp on the opposite side from the trail, hearing the motors of the jeeps laboring above them. And, after a time, the noise of the motors stopped, so they knew by then Villalonga's soldiers had found the body of Peter's horse and whatever the kites and buzzards had left of the shattered carcass of Juan's. From then on it would only be a matter of time before they found the place where one left the trail to come down to the camp. So, without Jacinto's having to say anything, they all started force-marching, on the double, until Peter was covered with sweat and staring at Father Pío. The old priest went as fast as the rest. Faster than most.

Behind them, the noise of the motors started up again.

When they had put them behind them finally, faded them out of time, they could see the jungle before them. Here, where they were, they had to cross a marsh to get into it. Peter looked at the marsh mud. Then suddenly, he sat down in that sticky, black mud. It came up to his waist. He lay down in it, rolled over. Stood up again. What he looked like they couldn't put a name to.

"Now, what the devil?" Pepe said.

"Defense against insects," Peter said. "When it dries I shall be armored. I saw the water buffalo do this in Indo-China."

"Is there any place you haven't been, son?" Father Pío said.

"Yes," Peter said. "Heaven."

"Nor hell either," the old priest said.

Peter stopped smiling.

"I wouldn't bet on that one, Padre," he said.

Going through the jungle was as bad as before except that this time the bugs couldn't get at him. The sweat ran off him in rivers, plowing furrows through the mud on his face. But he stooped and clawed up hunks of fetid jungle earth and patted them back over the bare spots. He got through the jungle like that almost unbitten. Then they were out of it again and at the foot of the Sierras again, but at a place other than the old camp. Looking up, he saw they were much closer to Zopocomapetl than before. Almost at the foot of it, in fact. Where they were now the trail was very definite, worn by many years of use. When Peter mentioned that to Pepe, the second officer said:

"Yes. There is an Indian village called Xochua about an hour's climb from here. We shall stop there to rest."

"Isn't that dangerous?" Peter said.

"No. The Indians never tell anything to Villalonga's soldiers. In fact, the troops of the National Army never see any Indians."

"Why not?" Peter said.

"The Tluscola are a proud people. Unlike those dirty fisher Indians down on the coast, they do not share their women. Additionally, they do not relish having their heads cracked upon with gun butts. So now, when the troops come up here, long before they arrive, the Tluscolas have gone. And when they go, they leave not even an ear of corn in their houses for the soldiers to eat. At first, Villalonga's brigands used to throw down the houses in their rage; but to throw down houses built of stone and adobe calls for too much work. And Costa Verdians do not like work, amigo!"

"Who does?" Peter said. "They don't run from you, then?"

"No. Juan made it absolutely clear that he would shoot any man who touched a Tluscola woman. So now we have been among them many times, and they know their daughters are safe. Which is a point they are very strict about. A Tluscola girl who is not a virgin when she comes to her marriage bed is put to death in a sickening fashion. That is, if the new husband was not himself responsible for her loss of virginity prior to the ceremony. In that case, they pardon the offense, holding that the marriage removes the sin. They killed all the unmarried women of Xochunga after the soldiers of Our Generous Benefactor swept through that town. Because they were just, they acknowledged that the loss of their virginity was not the girls' fault; they killed them not as they usually do in such cases, but quickly and mercifully. The married women they merely gave a ceremonial beating and let it go at that. But the young men of Xochunga, having no girls to marry, had to leave that pueblo; and for a while, there was trouble among the Tluscolas."

"You said that they killed the young women mercifully," Peter said. "How do they kill them if *las chicas* have merely been generous and donated a small portion thereof, of their own free will?"

Pepe shuddered.

"*Hombre*—let us not speak of that!" he said.

When they came into Xochua, the Indians greeted them with grave courtesy. At least until they saw that Father Pío was with them. Then they ignored Peter and the rest completely, and clustered around the old priest, dropping to their knees before him.

Father Pío blessed them, talking to them in the harsh grunts and gutturals of their own language.

The Chief of the Indians came up to Peter.

"You new Cacique?" he said in Spanish.

"No," Peter said, "why?"

"You most tall," the Chief said. "More tall than any. The other Cacique was tall. Dead now, no? The great hawk of the thunder kill him, yes?"

"Yes," Peter said.

"Who Cacique now?" the Chief said.

"That one," Peter said. "The Comrade with the yellow eyes."

The Chief looked at Jacinto. Looked back at Peter.

"Better you Cacique," he said.

"Why?" Peter said.

"Know that one. Crazy like sick wolf. Bad. I talk you, not him."

"Talk then," Peter said.

"You stay here, four-five days."

"Now look, Chief—" Peter said.

"You stay here four-five days," the Chief said.

"Why?" Peter said.

"Many dead. No big medicine said over them to bury, *sabes*? Many *bebes* without the good water on their heads. Many young people not married in church together, girls big belly, and Padre Pío no take away the sin. Four-five days. Yes? Padre said he your prisoner. Say ask Cacique."

"Chief," Peter said, "I've got news for you. I'm a prisoner just like the good Padre. And we cannot stay here. The soldiers would come. Bad. Screw all the girls. Then you would have to kill them, no?"

"I think better we kill the soldiers," the Chief said.

"You've got something there, Chief," Peter said.

"Soldiers come, we hide you, hide us," the Chief said. "Never find."

"Look, Chief, all I can do is to ask the Jefe. Then I'll come back and tell you. Of accord?"

"*De acuerdo,*" said the old chief.

Peter walked over to where Pepe and Jacinto stood.

"What was the old buzzard talking with you about?" Pepe said.

"He wants us to stay four or five days," Peter said, "so that Padre Pío can police up the place. Seems there has been nocturnal frolicking around. Girls big belly, the old boy says. Look, Pepe, I thought that was a hanging offense . . ."

"Worse," Pepe said, "but all he means is that they've only been married by Indian ceremonies and not in the Church. Besides, you did not understand me, Peter. They do not kill young people for fornication. They make them get married. It is only when a girl is formally engaged to a young man, and on their wedding night he finds that—due to the activities of another rapid type—you could drive a jeep up it, that the poor thing is put to death . . ."

"What do they do with the male offender?"

"If they can catch him, they alter him. But usually the girls don't tell . . ."

"Jacinto," Peter said, "about our staying here——"

Jacinto turned very slowly from where he had been staring off across the village square. His yellow eyes came back from farther than that. From towering heights. Immense depths. From heaven, maybe. Or, more likely, hell.

"All right," he said.

"What!" Peter and Pepe said together.

"You heard me. I said 'Of accord.' "

That was one of the good times. After he got used to how an Indian house smelled. After he got over the shock of opening a door and having a dead man grin at him with immense yellow teeth. In spite of the fleas.

They took the dead man away the next morning, after Padre Pío had told the Indians that he wouldn't christen babies, perform marriages, hear confession, or say Mass unless they consented to bury their dead properly. The burial ceremonies were very colorful, so Peter asked Jacinto to give him back at least one of the four cameras he had had in his saddle roll and which they had confiscated along with his carbine. Jacinto gave them all back without a word.

"What's got into him?" Peter said to Pepe.

"I do not know. Father Pío said once that he would become a great criminal or a saint. It frightens me. I prefer him as a criminal. When he is blustering about, threatening to shoot people, I know how to handle him; but this quietness, this saintly mood—*Dios mío*—who knows what he will do next?"

The following morning they found out.

Peter came over to where the Indians stood, silent and rapt, looking at the old Chief. Slowly, powerfully, the old man was swinging a rawhide whip. It sang through the air, whistled, bit. Peter heard something that sounded like a moan. He pushed his way through the crowd. The girl was young. She was hanging by her wrists, which had been bound with rawhide thongs to a crossbar set on two forked poles, high enough so that her whole body swung beneath it. She was naked. And the whipping had been going on for some time, because she was striped and bleeding from her heels to her neck. She was thickset and not particularly pretty. She smelled of blood, and even more strongly of that nauseous odor that the gray beans they ate gave to the Indians' sweat. That and the smell of unwashed female and the stench of fear came over and took Peter in the face. He retched; but he came on, stood before the Chief.

"Why?" he said.

"She lay down for white man," the Chief said, "for him of the yellow eyes."

"You mean to beat her to death?" Peter said.

"No. Just five more. Then we sit her on the stick."

"You sit her on the stick?" Peter said.

"Sí," the Chief said, and pointed with the butt of the whip.

Peter turned. There in the middle of the square a stake had been driven into the ground. It stood all of thirty inches high. It had been sharpened into a spearpoint—that is, the top of it had. He hung there, staring at it.

"Law," the old Chief said. "Man steal, cut him off hand. Lie, split him tongue. Woman do that, we—"

"My God!" Peter said. "Chief—"

"Yes, tall Cacique?"

"You'll let me call Padre Pío first? Let her say her prayers before? After all—"

"Sí. De acuerdo," the Chief said.

Father Pío was something to see. He roared like a lion in Spanish and Tluscolan. He waved his arms, stamped his feet. Some of the things he said didn't come out of the Catechism.

"Savages!" he said. "Dolts! Idiots! How many times have I told you—"

"Law," the old Chief said. "She open legs for the white man."

"But she is not married!" Father Pío said. "I will fetch the white man and make him marry her."

"She engaged my son. You to marry them, today," the Chief said. "No good now. She come tell him what happen before."

"Which means she did not deceive him," Padre Pío said. "She told him before, Zochoa!"

"No difference. She lay down, open legs, bump bellies with the Cacique of the Yellow Eyes all night long and—"

"No!" the girl screamed suddenly, "it's a lie! A lie, Padre!"

"Son," Father Pío said, "lend me your shirt."

Peter took off his shirt and handed it to the priest. It was still mud-caked. But that didn't matter now.

Padre Pío gave the shirt to the old Chief.

"Have the favor to wrap her in this," he said, "so that I may speak to her. Her nakedness is an offense to my priesthood. Go on, cover her up!"

The Chief wrapped the girl in Peter's shirt. Padre Pío stepped up to her.

"Hija mía," he began in Spanish; "my daughter—the truth, now. What passed with thee?"

She told him. But in Tluscolan. As the old priest listened, he began to smile. Then to grin. Laughter twitched about his mouth. He covered it with his hand, but the rich, dark sound of his laughter came out between his fingers. By the time she had finished, he had tears in his eyes. But they were tears of mirth, not sorrow.

"Zochoa!" he said. "Call the council of the women. Have them take her into that house there and examine her. She swears that she is virgin still. That your son did not understand—that, in his rage, he would not listen to what she was really saying. Go on, call the women!"

The old Chief looked puzzled. He looked at Padre Pío.

"Do as I say, Zochoa!" Padre Pío said.

"Very well, Padre, I call them," Zochoa said.

And now, after the girl had been borne into the house amid a great gabbling of women, Peter saw the younger Indian men coming up the trail pushing Jacinto along ahead of them. His hands were tied behind his back and one of the Indians was pointing his own burp gun at him.

"I wonder," Peter said, "how many he killed before they took him?"

"None," Father Pío said, "or else he would not be alive now. They are very good at tricks, the Tluscola. It is likely that they made him empty his weapon into a pig or a goat disguised as a man, then took him before he could reload."

Peter could see the other guerrillas coming out of the other houses with the assault guns in their hands. Pepe put himself at the head of them and gave swift orders. The third officer, the one called Federico, repeated them.

"Father—" Peter said.

"Do not preoccupy yourself, Son Pedro," Father Pío said.

The Indians marched Jacinto into the square. They stood there all around him, waiting. The guerrillas made a wide circle around them, holding the machine pistols muzzle downward, not aiming them.

Pepe came over to where Peter and Padre Pío stood.

"What has he done?" he said.

"Don't know. Fornication. Rape. Or something else. Something worse, maybe," Peter said.

They waited. The women came out of the house. They

were mountains of flesh under their gray hair. The girl was with them. They had bathed her, dressed her in her wedding dress, put flowers in her hair. It was an ordinary wedding dress, bought, probably, in Ciudad Villalonga.

When they saw her dressed in white, the Indians set up a roar.

"What does it mean?" Peter said.

"That she has been vindicated," Padre Pío said.

The women, led by the girl herself, walked over to where the men were guarding Jacinto. When she was close enough, the girl leaned forward and spat into Jacinto's face.

The old Chief said something in Tluscolan. Peter didn't need to know what the words meant. The young Indians obeyed at once. They took out their knives and cut Jacinto loose.

"You see," Jacinto said, "I told you I did not touch her!"

The girl's head came back. Her laughter floated up, silvery and sure. The sky gave it back. The mountains. She ripped out a phrase. Then the Indians started laughing. All the square was loud with their laughter.

Father Pío's face was a sight to see. He didn't want to laugh, but he couldn't help it. His old lined, seamed, gnarled face fought his laughter, but the laughter won.

Jacinto stood there. His eyes were sick. He looked from one side to another.

"What says this woman?" Pepe roared. "Tell me, what does the woman say?"

"I say," the girl said, her Spanish heavy-voiced, but clear and sure, "that he is incapable. He is guilty, your friend, of intention. Only—"

"Shut up!" Jacinto howled.

"He is not a man," the girl said. "He tried. All night he tried, menacing me with his knife. But he could not. He is not a man. He tried. But his flesh failed him."

"Jacinto!" Pepe said. "Your pants!"

The guerrillas were laughing too now, shouting that phrase Jacinto had himself invented. "Your pants! Remove them that we may see what, if anything you have in them!"

Peter didn't laugh. He was too busy watching Jacinto's eyes. He saw them change. He started moving toward Jacinto. He was too late.

Jacinto uncoiled like a spring. Snatched a Bren gun from the nearest of his comrades. Whirled, the burp gun flattened against his hip, already flaming; and he, Peter, coming in on a long diagonal, already in midair in a flying tackle, saw Pepe crumple under that blast, his uniform smoking, jerking under the impact as half a clip tore into him; but Peter's arms were around Jacinto's neck and shoulder now, smashing him to the ground, and the gun still talking—but aimlessly now, stitching a line of holes across one of the houses high up under the roof until it bucked empty, and Jacinto swinging it out and sidewise with all his force so that red fire exploded inside Peter's head; and he heard or thought he heard or even dreamed as the sudden dark crashed down, Pepe's voice, fading, dying, choking, say:

"No! Let him go— Let him go— Do not kill him for—this——"

And Father Pío moving out between them and Jacinto's flying form, his arms outstretched in the form of the cross, very small and straight there on the mountainside, saying, his old voice infinitely weary:

"No, children. There has been already too much blood."

5.

Here, where they were now, there was not flatness anywhere and the mountain was honeycombed with caves. They used the caves to sleep in; but they were very damp and cold and uncomfortable so fires had to be kept going in them all night

long. There was plenty of water. It sprang from the rocks in
trickles and streams, ice-cold and clear. On one side of the
camp a cataract foamed down for two hundred meters making a noise like thunder, so loud and so constant that after a
day it faded out of consciousness as traffic noises do to one
whose window opens on a busy street. Beside the big cataract there was a small one, with a fall of only three meters
that made a lovely shower bath when the sun was out in the
middle of the day.

Peter was under it, its icy needles making him dance and
roar, while the clothes he had already washed lay drying in
the sun with the rocks on them to keep them from blowing
away. The four guards that Federico, the new commander,
had placed over him and Father Pío lay on the ground and
smoked cigarettes. And now Father Pío came out of the cave
and walked over to the little shower.

"Cleanliness is next to godliness," he said.

Peter came out of the cataract and began to walk about,
slapping his body with his hands. After a time the wind
and the sun dried him, so he picked up his clothes, blown
dry and stiff, and put them on. The old priest sat down beside him. Peter looked at that ancient gargoyle face, seeing
that it was lined and sad.

"What passes with you, Father?" he said.

"I should not have laughed," Padre Pío said. "It was a sin
to laugh."

"But very natural," Peter said. "He made such a thing of
his masculinity. Have you noticed, Father, how often men
give an exaggerated importance to what they doubt in themselves? What truly they do not have?"

"Jacinto is not effeminate," Father Pío said. "What he is is
wounded."

"Wounded how?" Peter said.

"In his soul, profoundly. Tell me, Son Pedro, what do you
know of psychology?"

"Nothing. Or almost. And I doubt what little I do know."

"That is your wound, Pedro. That you doubt all things."

"You think I like it, Father?"

"No. I know that no man of your intelligence would move in the cold wilderness, bemused by shadows, sickened by emptiness, if he could enjoy the warmth and comfort of Faith. As you will, one day."

"Don't make book on that, Father," Peter said.

"What did you say, son? I have no English," the old priest said.

"Nothing. A stupidity. You think that Jacinto lives?"

"Sí. He may even have joined one of the other guerrilla bands in another part of the Sierras. But I doubt that. He will run alone, now. He is like a crazy wolf. His capacity for survival is great. I wish I could have saved him. For his place should have been in a monastery. In a contemplative order. One where the vows are of silence, work, and poverty. Because, you see, son, he has a vocation of chastity."

"Ho!" Peter said. "You mean he has a vocation of impotency, don't you, Father? Combined with two or three more. Murder, for instance."

"A little more charity, son. I think that marriage and the begetting of sons are not for Jacinto. I think that when he approaches a woman the vision of his sister the night he found her fills up his mind, freezes his normally ardent blood. Hence, for him, a contemplative order—"

"For him the gallows," Peter said, "for having murdered poor Pepe!"

"Son," Father Pío said, "Pepe forgave him before he died."

"Pepe was a bigger man than I," Peter said. "I had grown fond of Pepe. Of them all, he had the most heart, and the highest degree of intelligence. This band is finished now, you know. Without either Juan or Pepe they have no chance. I only hope the other bands have better luck, though I wonder if it will help matters or make them worse for the Castristas to win. But speaking of bands, Father—do you know where Federico took those twelve men this morning?"

"No," Father Pío said, "but you do, do you not, Son Pedro?"

"Yes. They have gone to raid Ciudad Villalonga itself. To blow up an assembly plant of trucks that belongs to the

Dictator. On the outskirts of the city. A monumental piece of folly. They will not survive it. Directly contrary to Juan's policy, which was to keep moving, try to link up with the other bands, gather recruits until they could strike in strength, signaling at that moment the clandestine bands within the city to rise up and help them. Father—"

"Yes, son?"

"Tomorrow, if they have not returned, we must escape, you and I."

"You think it is possible, son?"

"Yes. The caves. We must go casually into the third one. It has an exit."

"Do they not know that?" Father Pío said.

"Yes," Peter said, "but they will discount it. You see, the exit comes out under the big cataract. They will not believe that you and I will risk being swept away."

The old priest looked at him.

"Is the risk very great?"

"Enormous. It curdles my guts to even think of it. I would not attempt it alone. But with you, Old One—"

"With me, what?" Padre Pío said.

"It is a thing that you have. Luck, maybe. Or the Grace of God. If there is a God—I wouldn't know. Only with you and for you, it works. With you, I shall go without fear. Without too much fear, in any event. Because it can be done, only if one is not afraid to the extent that paralyzes the will. One must not look down. One must only look up—"

"And pray," Father Pío said.

"And pray. Which is your department, Father. That's all I ask of you, that you keep a hot wire plugged in with Upstairs. Because that's not my line—my prayers are of first-class lead. And go up about as fast. Will you try it, Old One?"

"Speak of it," Father Pío said.

"The exit comes out under the big falls. Only the water does not cling to the rocks, but springs out from them so that there is a space of two meters where only the spray strikes. In that space there is a ledge thirty centimeters wide on which one can walk. That ledge is of an utter vileness of slipperiness, and is of shale rock that may crumble beneath us. Below it, there is nothing. Below it there is only death."

"For the little children of the good God there is never *only* death, son."

"As you will, Father. I have stolen two knives. I stole a pistol, too; but I put it back, because to cross that ledge even a pistol will be too heavy to carry. You will carry the two canteens—empty, because water itself weighs a barbarity, and every gram we don't have to carry will help. I will dig handholds in the rock wall which is of shale, and soft. When I take away my hand, you must put yours in the place I have left. Like that we will proceed five meters until we have come out from under the waterfall. What we will find there, I do not know. I think there is a trail of a certain vileness going down. But whether it connects up with that ledge, I do not know. The only way to tell that is to try it. Will you, Father?"

"Of course, son," the old priest said. "And, son, before I forget, it was very brave of you to try to save Pepe as you did, attacking Jacinto with only your hands—"

"Less than you think," Peter said. "I was trained to fight with my hands. I led Commando raiding parties in Korea. I can kill a man with my bare hands, Father."

"And you consider this an accomplishment?" Father Pío said.

"No," Peter said. "It sickens me. And I could not do it now. I no longer have the will."

"Good. I am glad of that," Father Pío said.

Just before noon that next day, they saw Federico and the others coming up the trail. There had been twelve of them when they started out; now there were only nine. Peter and the guards went down to meet them.

"How went it, Freddie?" Peter said.

"Of a vile vileness," Federico said.

"Then this of the truck factory—"

"The factory? That went well. That was fine. That was enormous. Only—"

"Only what, Freddie?" Peter said.

"They wounded Roberto and Martin so badly I had to shoot them. But what is worse, that idiot Jaime allowed himself to be taken. By now they know of this place. Jaime is not one to resist torture very long. But that is not the worst."

"What is the worst, then?" Peter said.

"Our people within the city, hearing the explosions, rose up, thinking that the invasion had started. As we were leaving, we could hear the firing. And the screams. They were not coordinated. Nor prepared. By nightfall, our fifth column will have ceased to exist. And it is my fault! Mine! If I had listened to you, Pedro; if I had only listened to you!"

"Freddie," Peter said, "do not waste time blaming yourself. Now, it seems to me that once again, we must get out of here, move on—"

"No," Federico said.

"*Madre de Dios!* Are you mad?"

"No," Federico said.

"Then?" Peter said.

"I weary of running. I tire of being hunted like a beast. They know where we are. Let them come and take us—if they are willing to pay what it costs, which will be dear. Wili!"

"*Sí*, Jefe?" Guillermo said.

"Set up the machine guns. There before the caves—to cover that flank. The mortars a little higher. Comrades! I will now say a thing: If any of you, despite all our indoctrination, wishes to go to the little Father to confess and make your act of contrition, you have my permission, and my promise that you will not be punished for it. Since it is likely we shall all die, take what comfort you can—"

"Freddie, you are crazy!" Peter said, watching the two or three soldiers of the band who either sheepishly or defiantly headed for Father Pío's cave.

"Now, there is no chance, Peter. I am too tired. And they have the helicopters from your Navy's Aircraft Carriers scouting for them, now . . ."

Peter looked at him.

"I do not believe that," he said.

"Yet it is true," Federico said. "Your State Department is determined that Costa Verde shall not be another Cuba. Hence they have applied the formula that worked so well for you in Viet Nam: Your forces are 'technical advisers.' Technical advisers with copters that find us, guns that shoot us, napalm to roast us alive, bombs to spatter our guts. So, there is no chance now. If we leave here, we will be taken cheaply at little cost. Since die we must, let us make them pay high for our butchered, uneatable meat, with mountains of chopped loinsteak of their own. You and the little Vasco go into the caves when it starts, and only come out again when it is over, waving the white flag of surrender. That, Comrade Reporter, is an order."

"Freddie, you are either much man or a fool. Though I wonder if they are not usually the same thing."

"And I, Peter," Federico said.

Under the falls, the thunder of the water was so great that talking was impossible. Peter hung there, probing in a crevice of the rock with his knife. The spray was ice-cold. It stung like a thousand whiplashes. Every time he moved his feet they slipped out from under him and his gut turned over. But he hung on, digging handholds fifty centimeters apart. Then he saw that Father Pío was having a hard time stretching up to reach them, so he cut them lower and closer together, which made them better for the little priest, but difficult and dangerous for him. Finally he had to compromise by cutting two sets, which took twice as long. But he kept on cutting them, like that.

He ached all over, and his muscles were jerking from fatigue. They inched along that ledge like sodden spiders, spread out in a series of momentary crucifixions. Even through the mist, he could see Father Pío's lips moving in prayer.

But he had neither the time nor the strength for praying. He moved centimeter by centimeter, dying a little each time his foot slipped, being resurrected when his grip held in the downward-slanted handhold he had cut into the rotten rock. It took them two hours to cross that five meters. Then Peter hung there, seeing the place where the ledge had come to an abrupt end and beyond that the sheer drop of fifty meters down crumbling perpendicular shale rock faces that no living thing larger than an insect could have managed, and even an insect with appalling difficulty. And across that, an obscene, unspeakable, vile vileness of an unjumpable three meters away the beginning of the trail he had seen the day before.

He hung there with the icy mist on his face mingling with the lava like sulphuric tears and a great wave of profanity choking in his throat which he had no longer had the breath to say. He looked at Father Pío. The little priest bowed his head.

"It is the will of God, Son Pedro," he said.

Going back was easier. They already had their handholds. They got back into the cave, soaked to their bones' marrow, their teeth chattering like castanets. Crawled to the fire. The water in their clothes made steam rise up chokingly past their nostrils. They lay there without talking. The warmth stole into them; the tiredness spread out, out, until abruptly it ended time. Unattended, the fire burned itself out.

What wakened them was the cough and the thump of the mortars.

Because he was first of all a reporter, Peter came out of the cave. He crawled out of it on his belly, with the Leica with the 130-mm. telescopic lens in his hands, and the Nikon with the normal F 1.4 lens slung around his neck and resting on his back as he crawled. At his side he had the spring-wound robot camera that could shoot bursts of ten or twelve shots, making a series. He had left the Rolleiflex in the cave because it was too heavy and bulky for this kind of action.

Federico had been right. He was the last of the band who had been trained under the Russians in Cuba, and his use of the topography was masterly. They had caught Villalonga's troops in the open on the plateau below the caves and the slaughter was sickening. Peter pinpointed the long lens on one man, caught the exact instant of his death; the expression of pure disbelief on his face as a slug tore into him. He swept their faces, caught fear forever in silver salts; immobilized a falling body in midair; froze horror, froze pain in a series of shots better than any he had ever taken before. Then, as they whirled, running, he switched to the robot, capturing the attitudes of flight; the wild antics of men trying to stretch their tiny allotment of breath for an instant longer—an hour more under the sun.

Then they were all gone. And Federico threw one more mortar shell among the grotesque sprawl and seep and twist of the bodies, dismembering them; making sure that no one of them would rise. Then he turned to Peter, his teeth flashing white amid the blackness of his beard.

"What a slaughter!" he said.

"Now will you go?" Peter said.

"No. These were bait for the trap. The rest wait below to take us."

"Comrade—" Peter said.

"Sí, amigo?" Federico said.

"May I photograph you—and your men? This I think is a thing for history. Such men as you and yours should not be forgot, whatever the justice of your cause. May I?"

"Of course," Federico said.

They waited. Twenty minutes later, they heard the heavy roar of aircraft motors coming in.

Peter stood near the door of the cave, looking up. The two Vought Corsairs, the Mustang, and the fat-bellied P-47, went over once; then they barreled up in a climbing turn as tight as though they had been tied together on a string. He could see them, very high now: the Corsairs blue-black against the sky, but the Mustang and the Thunderbird silver; and he, waiting, caught them in the telescopic lens, as they peeled off, started down.

He stood there, shooting his pictures, rock-solid as they

came in, their props mist-silver, the leading edges of their wings aflame with the multiple spluttering jet-torch of their guns; the rockets hissing out of the racks and coming ruler-straight for the mouths of the caves; and the explosions hammering, throwing up earth and rock, and he, standing there, babbling like the fool he didn't even know he was being: "Oh, brother; what a shot! What a shot! Come on down, you buzzards! Closer! That's it! Oh, baby, what a sweetheart of a shot!"

And they, those well-trained guerrillas, who could have stood off an army, breaking now, scattering, because nothing is harder to face than being strafed from the air; nothing, not even tanks, gives a man a greater feeling of helplessness; and he, photographing them as they ran, caught the whole thing as it was, so that, afterward, he was never able to look at those photographs again.

The planes whining up, the sound of their motors thinning, then coming down again in a bellow that wracked sound out of existence; and the fat black bombs detaching themselves from under the wings and striking, bursting, sending up not the explosive shriek and tear of shrapnel but a soft *plofff* of pure liquid flame.

Peter saw the men turn into torches trailing fire behind them as they ran. Saw, and photographed them as they fell on their stomachs, or on their backs, their legs arching back, their arms flung out as they twisted sidewise in a circle like flies sprayed with insecticide; screaming with opened, blackened mouths; only their screams were lost in the bull-bellow, prop-whistle, tearing-up soaring snarl of the motors, in the hammer of the bombs; the teletype sentence of death the wing guns were dictating into the mouths of the caves.

Then, higher up, he saw the Cr 47s—the old Douglass DC 3s—open their guts and defecate parachutists across the sky. He got that picture, too; but he knew that it was time to get out of there, especially since Villalonga's pilots were calling their shots now, placing load after load of napalm directly into the mouths of the caves.

He went back into the cave to where the old priest knelt

in prayer, jerked the old man to his feet and started toward the mouth of the cave; but not getting there because the explosion flattened them both and the rolling billow of flame licked above their prone bodies with a heat that had to be felt to be believed and was not entirely believable even then.

They started crawling toward the exit, toward the hopeless opening under the falls. Got there and edged onto the ledge while their burning clothes hissed and sizzled out under the spray; and, hanging there, then inching out for the second time along that ledge, and again reaching that dead end, standing there until they saw the planes heading back toward Zopocomapetl; the fighters in a tight, professional V above the transports; the transports lumbering awkwardly, fighting each other's propwash, their formation ragged; but all of Miguel Villalonga's air force heading homeward now, their job well done.

Peter and Padre Pío stayed on that ledge for two and a half hours after Peter had seen the head of one of the paratroopers thrust through the spray, hanging there until the ache in their fingers, their arms, their backs, got to be worse than their fear, then they went back into the cave. The napalm had burned itself out long ago. They were alone. The paratroopers had gone back down the trail, bearing the bodies of their own troops and those of the Castristas with them.

They didn't talk. They filled the canteens and started walking. Halfway down the trail a Navy helicopter stopped and hovered over their heads.

Peter flagged it down. The two pilots jumped out. Stood there, looking at them.

"My God, it's Father Pío!" one of them said.

"And Peter Reynolds," Peter said. "Look, gentlemen, I don't know whether hitchhiking is within regulations, but if it is, may I respectfully request permission to come aboard?"

"Why sure, Mr. Reynolds," the pilot said. "We were sent out to look for you when that fracas started. Seems your father put in a call to the Senator from Massachusetts; he blasted our Ambassador down here, and he blew the whistle on Captain Andrews. Said there'd be hell to pay if you got yours—"

"I see," Peter said. "I suppose there must be some way to convince my old man that I'm crowding forty, but I haven't found it yet. Anyhow——"

The co-pilot of the Sikorsky was staring at all the cameras that Peter was carrying.

"Did you get any good shots, sir?" he said.

Peter stopped.

"Thanks, Commander," he said, "and not just for asking. Look, Sir—I'm going to give you all these rolls. Fly them out to the carrier, will you? Because Miguelito's goon squad will confiscate them sure as hell if I try to bring them in. Tell your Captain that it would be in the public interest if he got this film to New York. Tell him he can make copies of any or all of it for Naval Intelligence, but ask him to see that my paper gets this stuff. I need my job, Sir—"

"Roger. Can do," the pilot said.

On the flight back in the chopper, Peter reloaded the cameras. Better that the goon squad had something to snatch. Because even the apehood in which their minds labored was capable of suspicion if they found the cameras empty. By the time he had finished that, they were over the town.

The refinery fire was out. The British aircraft carrier stood out to sea. The American one had steam up. There was a long white yacht tied up to the quay. *La Flor del Mar*. The *Seaflower*. The beautiful craft The Leader used on his justly famous fishing expeditions. On the last one he had broken the world's record for blue marlin taken on a regulation line.

Peter pointed at the aircraft carriers.

"Why?" he shouted above the whacking rattle of the copter's blades.

"No further need—revolution's over!" the co-pilot said.

"That's what you think, friend!" Peter said.

"What did you say?" the co-pilot shouted.

"I said it's not," Peter called back, "because even if only a certain party I know is left, he'll——"

"What are you saying, Son Pedro?" Father Pío said. He was close enough to Peter not to have to shout.

Peter said it over again in Spanish.

"What man is that?" Father Pío said.

Peter's mouth grinned, but his eyes didn't.

"Me, Father," he said. "When they knocked off Freddie, they paralyzed my other cheek. The one I used for turning purposes."

"I do not understand you, Pedro," Father Pío said.

"Don't worry about it, Father; I don't either."

The helicopter drifted downward toward la Plaza de la Liberación, black with people, in the heart of the town.

Book Two

THE CITY

6.

When it was over and they had let him go—after having held him long enough to rush those quite-blank films over to the police laboratory and confirm his absolutely untrue statement that he hadn't taken any pictures, had been too scared during the battle to poke his head out of the cave, even retaining him another half-hour after that to make him shoot up a roll of twelve with the Rollei of their triumph, which included the prize-winning shot of the Dictator, Miguel Villalonga, in crisp tropical whites, looking down at the pile of bodies in the plaza, while all unknown to him a vulture perched on the cornice above his head—Peter got into a taxi, exchanging as he did so a wave of hands with Father Pío, who was being borne away to the Archbishop's palace in a limousine whose luxury was more than a little mundane, and drove straight to the little flat he had rented a month ago, the day Judith had arrived.

He had, miraculously, his key, and the mass of codfon bills that were to have been the down payment of Father Pío's ransom; so he was able not only to pay the taxi driver but also to ease by Concha, La Portera, without her seeing him in his present bearded, filthy state. He opened the door with his key and entered that little flat, so like and so different from all the dozens of other little flats he had rented for longer or shorter periods in so many Latin American capitals; and not even too different from the ones he'd had in Europe, Africa, Asia, except that it was newer, less time-worn.

When Judith didn't come flying at the sound of the opened door, he tiptoed into the bedroom. But she wasn't there, either. So he tried the knob of the bathroom door. It was empty, too. He walked all over the flat, looking around. Her clothes still hung in the closet. The vanity was covered as always with the jars and flasks of female sorcery. In the drawers were all the bras she still didn't need, all the filmy triangular wisps designed not so much for concealment as for provocation, made, as he had sworn more than once, to be ripped off her. The perfumed mist of negligees, slips, even those night-gowns she never slept in and those stockings woven of cob-webs and mist. But Judith wasn't there. That perfume of hers, *Peut-être*, that could still knot his guts at the first whiff, hung heavy and still on the air. But no Judy—no Judy at all.

He went back into the bathroom and answered the more pressing calls of nature. Washed his face and neck, lathered his stiff, black beard, picked up his Rolls razor—which, al-though it was a safety razor, had a permanent blade and a mechanism for sharpening it, thus eliminating the risk, in-herent in his profession, of running out of blades in places where you couldn't find any, or more frequently the places where they were impossible to shave with after you had found them—and stopped dead, staring at it, because the blade was gone.

"I wonder where the hell she's put it," he muttered. Then he frowned, shook his head. This wasn't like Judy. She was meticulous about small things. He had, of course, raised un-holy hell with her on more than one occasion for using his razor to shave her legs—largely as a matter of maintaining his position as lord and master, because the silken, almost invisible white blonde fuzz on Judy's legs certainly did less damage to the blade's edge than his barbed-wire beard did —but this was the first time she had ever failed to put it back. He searched for it, but he was too tired to do more than go through the motions, especially since, because he had spent his entire life, including his childhood, traveling, he had long since learned to carry two of every irreplaceable item. So he dug out the second blade, honed and stropped it to the required degree of keenness, and shaved.

He got into the shower, turned on the water, soaped himself all over and stepped under the spray. What ran off him could have been used to fill a fountain pen; so he stepped out of the area of the spray, reached for the soap to lather himself again. But he squeezed it a little too hard, and it shot from his hand in a hard, flat trajectory to land, as far as he could judge, behind the lavabo, the basin.

Swearing, he stepped out of the shower, got down on his hands and knees, pushed his right hand behind the column of the lavabo and groped for the soap. But his fingers touched something hard and cold, smeared, his tactile sense told him, with a thick, viscous substance. He drew it out. Knelt there, holding it.

It was the blade of his razor. The safety guard had been wrenched violently aside. The blade was covered with blood.

He sat down on the edge of the tub, holding it in the palm of his hand. He sat there, looking at it; and, because he knew Judith Lovell, knew in painful and complete detail her history, the palsied shaking in his limbs rose in waves through his body until his stomach knotted and he vomited, spewing forth the yellowish bile that was all he could throw up because he hadn't eaten anything in close to forty-eight hours.

Then he dropped to his knees, contorted his wet, slippery body into the little space between the bidet and the lavabo. Looking upward, he could see the whole back of the basin—which should have been flush with the tiled wall, but, because it had been installed by Latins, naturally wasn't—dripped thick, ropy, slowly coagulating blood.

He got up. Stared at the bidet, the toilet. They were spotless. There was no blood anywhere except behind the washbasin. He stretched out a hand that shook so that he had a hard time closing his grip, took a bath towel, dried himself. Went into the bedroom, moving slowly, like a sleepwalker. Opened the drawers, took out underwear, socks, a shirt, a handkerchief. Dressed himself in the same somnolent detachment until he was clad in shirt and pants, but barefoot still. Then it hit him. He doubled in half, clutching his middle with both hands, lifted up his head and howled:

"Simple! Oh very simple, Padre! You hear me? Just like falling off a log!"

Then he was off: running toward the kitchen, and getting there, yanking the interior phone, the one that connected directly with the *porteria,* off the hook and screaming into it:

"Concha! Concha! Answer me for the love of God!"

"*Diga?*" Concha said.

"Concha," he said, "the Señorita; where is she? What the devil has passed here?"

"Ay, Señor!" Concha wailed. "The poor little thing! She is in the hospital! In Our Lady of the Remedies! She—"

But he had slammed the phone down and was yanking on his shoes, socks, a tie, tearing on his jacket, transferring his keys, his billfold, his passport, identity card, the sodden mass of bills, to the pockets of his lightweight suit, and going out of there, taking the stairs four at a time going down, only to meet Concha coming up them.

"Ay, Señor!" she wept. "Ay, Señor, if you could have seen her! Standing over the lavabo with your razor in her hand! And the blood! Ay, yai, yai, the blood! Never have I seen so much! Not even at the bullfight! *Ay, Madre de Dios! Ay, Señor Nuestro!* The blood! The blood!"

He caught the fat, greasy wrists.

"Why? In God's name, Concha; why?"

"The radio, Señor; The radio! It announced the great battle, although it didn't have to, because we could hear the explosions from here and see the airplanes diving and the smoke coming up. And afterwards the announcer said—he said—"

"What, woman? What, Concha? Tell me!"

"That you were dead, Señor! That you and the saintly Father Pío had been killed by the Reds! I thought about the Señorita when I heard that—knowing how nervous she is.

And I was thanking the Sainted Mother that the Señorita knows no Spanish, when he said it over again—in English!"

Peter stared at her.

"Why?" he said. "Why should he do that?"

"I do not know, truly, Señor. But Mario, my son, says it is because The Leader wished your Marines on that aircraft carrier out there to hear and come to his aid. I cannot swear he said the same words, but he repeated your name and that of Father Pío, twice—"

"Figures," Peter said. "Go on, Concha!"

"So I came up here. The door was open and—"

"Thank you, Concha," Peter said.

"I—I cleaned up. I do not know why. I thought I had removed it all, the blood. Only—"

"You did just fine." Peter edged past her.

"Señor, wait!"

Peter stopped.

"I called the hospital ten minutes ago. She is alive, but in the gravest of danger. But when she sees you, Señor, she will recover! I know it! What a great love! What enormous pride must the Señor have! To be envied by all men because of the beauty unequaled of his wife; and knowing additionally that she, this celebrity more famous than any other, this star of the camera, this luminary of the silver screen prefers to die rather than to live without him. What an enormous thing!"

Peter stood there listening to Concha exercising the vocabulary she'd gotten out of the fan magazines, which are absolutely as bad in Spanish as they are in English, and studying her face as she said all that. Then his head came back, his mouth opened. Laughter came out of him. Ripped out of him with the sound of tearing.

He mastered it, whirled, and ran down the stairs.

"Poor man!" Concha said. "The shock has deranged his mind . . ."

He sat there beside the bed, looking at Judith. Her hair was spread out over the pillow. It and the pillow and her face, and even her lips now, were all the same color: white.

Her eyebrows and lashes were only a little darker, the palest possible ash blonde, so that to achieve the platinum shade that other actresses had to murder their hair with peroxide to obtain, Judith merely had to sit in the sun a couple of hours a day, a thing she loved to do, anyhow.

He leaned forward suddenly, staring at her throat; at that thick collar of gauze wrapped around it. Leaned back, looked at the doctor. "My God!"

"She wasn't playing games," the doctor said in perfect, unaccented American.

"I thought—her wrists," Peter said. "Usually—"

"When they don't really mean it. Your girl did, Mr. Reynolds. After the fourth transfusion—she's had five now— twenty minutes after we put the call for donors out over the radio, the line stretched all around four blocks, hundreds of people who're going to spend the rest of their lives bragging about how they gave Judith Lovell the exact drop of blood that saved her life—she woke up and raved a bit. From what she said, I gather she hasn't had a happy existence—up until now. With you, yes. Seems to regard you as her salvation. Awfully dependent upon you, isn't she?"

"She's nuts," Peter said.

"You'd better pray she stays that way," the doctor said.

"I do," Peter said. "Every night."

He went on looking at her.

She stirred a little. Said, in her normal, clipped Back Bay accent:

"Pe-tah."

"Yes, Judy?" Peter said.

Her voice trailed off into a broken jumble. Peter looked at the doctor. At that type-form of the young, upper class Hispano-American, complete to the pencil-line mustache. Until he opened his mouth. Then what came out was New Yorkese.

"Doctor—is she out of danger?"

"I'm afraid the answer to that one is no, Mr. Reynolds."

"Good God!" Peter said.

"Amen. She made a beauty of a try, Reynolds. Missed the carotid by the thickness of a hair. Played old hell with a whole series of major veins. Incidentally, unless she can find an absolutely miraculous plastic surgeon, she's out of the motion pictures for good. I took nine stitches in that gash. And the scar isn't going to be exactly a joy forever."

"So now what do we do?"

"We wait, Mr. Reynolds."

"Oh, hell—call me Peter, will you? Because, if I know my Judy, once she starts talking, what you've been indulging in, listening to her, was a sort of nonvisual voyeurism. You now know more about me than my mother ever did, so why keep your distance? Besides, for saving Judy, you automatically head the list of my friends for life. Anything you ask me, if I've got it, it's yours."

"All right, Peter. Incidentally, my name's Vince. Vicente Gomez. Only the types at Harvard Med cut that down to Vince the first week. What I was going to say is that quite a lot may depend on your actions when she wakes up. I'm not exactly sold on psychiatry, but there does seem to be some there—a deep-seated guilt complex; even, I'd venture, if the term didn't sound so goddam phony, a kind of a death wish . . ."

"My slant is that Judy sort of extirpated the phoniness with her do-it-yourself surgery, Doctor."

"Exactly. And she made several half-intelligible references to a Doctor Dekov. Is that—"

"Doctor Leon Dekov, the psychiatrist? Yes, Vince. And, before you ask: She was in his clinic a year. Self-committed. Voluntarily. For nervous depression—after one of several attempts to pull a caper like this."

"All right. I'm through asking questions. But I should like to make what ought to be a completely unnecessary pitch—"

"Pitch away, Vinco."

"When she regains consciousness, you'd better pour it on, Peter. Rid her of her suspicion—about this she was highly articulate—that you're tired of her, that she's a burden to you. If she's only a quarter right, it's you who's nuts, not she. Even from the standpoint of altruism toward the general public, you can't let something that looks and is built like

Judith die. Let her get to sixty, boy. Let that glorious frame get to be just a memory even to her; then it won't be too bad. But now, God in Heaven, what a waste!"

Peter looked at him.

"You mean she's still in danger of dying?"

"I mean that if you don't convince her that you love the ground she walks on, she'll try this again. Or something more effective. At the moment, I believe that seeing that you're still among those present will snap her out of this one."

Doctor Gomez had a meal sent up from the hospital's kitchen for Peter, but he couldn't eat it. He got a little of it down; but then his stomach knotted up on him and wouldn't let the rest of it pass. He sat there watching Judith for the better part of two hours. One of the nursing sisters stayed with him. Vince looked in every quarter of an hour.

Still, when it happened, he was caught unaware. He was gazing out of the window; not really even listening to the sister's account of how Ciudad Villalonga happened to have this absolutely top-flight A-Number-One hospital, equipped with every piece of modern medical equipment that money could buy.

"So when the Reds shot our Great Leader," the sister said, "he was brought into the hospital we had then. Here, on the same site. But it was of an almost unimaginable badness. Señor, he came close to dying. In fact, he would have died, had not Luis Sinnombre, whom some say is his brother, conceived of the idea of putting him in an airplane and flying him up to the Clinic of the Brothers Mayo in your great country, Señor. When he came back, restored except for that limp he still has, which will not permit him to dance— he who loved dancing so!—he had the old hospital razed to the ground and built this one. He spent a fortune! A thousand millions, it is said. Why—"

"Yes, Sister?" Peter said. "Go on. I'm listening."

But behind him there was no sound at all. He turned and saw Judith's eyes. They were wide open, staring at him. At first they were blank and unfocused. Then they cleared.

A little pinpoint of light—reflected, perhaps, from the window behind Peter—got into them. It was very hard-edged, definite and bright. Then it splintered; broke into slivers like the facets of a diamond. Went molten, liquid; walling out the dead-level, still-blue smoke of her gaze behind a wash of crystal, shivering upon her lashes, trembling in fragile resistance to the whole ponderous downward pull of the world.

Her mouth came open; her snow-colored lips, whiter now than the rest of her face, made a pitiful, babbling blur that he couldn't look at, and couldn't stop looking at. He could see that what they were trying to shape into sound was his name; but they couldn't manage it.

He got up slowly, crossed to her, bent and put his mouth on them, on snowflutter, on ice, on the stench of disinfectants, on near-death.

He heard the click of the sister's heels as she fled down the hall.

When Vince came into the room, he was sitting in the chair by the bed, while Judith held his big hand with both of hers to her open, uncontrollably quivering mouth, and blessed it with her tears.

When he had retrieved his hand, which he managed to do only after she had sunk back into sleep again, he left the hospital, and started toward Pam-Pam, that curious quick-lunch chain that had jumped the ocean from Paris and proliferated all over Latin America. The food there was a trifle less uneatable than it was in the other cafés, tabernas, cantinas, and restaurantes. He still wasn't hungry, but he knew he had to eat something. But, before he could order, Tim O'Rourke, *Time-Life's* Latin American man, with whom he had been engaging in absolutely pitiless warfare for close to twelve years now, came into the place, caught him by both lapels and jerked him to his feet.

"C'mon," Tim said, "we're going to Les Ambassadeurs. It's on me. Deductible. Business expense. Interviewing a celebrity."

"Put that way, you've got me, Timmy, me b'y," Peter said.

"I can't afford Les Ambassadeurs. And I could use some food . . ."

"I hope it chokes you, you bastard," Tim said. "Now, come on."

"So," Tim said, "you think the revolution's not over?"

"I don't think," Peter said. "I know."

"Why not?" Tim said.

"Villalonga. You think they're going to quit with him still in power?"

"No," Tim said, "but they'd better hurry. If they want to have the pleasure of doing Miguelito in, I mean. I'd make book on some of his own friends knocking him off first."

"Why?" Peter said.

"You got all night? Ten million reasons. Finance for one. He demands and gets kickbacks from everything that operates in this monkey's paradise from a bootblack stand on up. Result? Just look in any direction. United Fruit's closing its office here, end of the month. The Verdian Hilton's losing money hand over fist; tourists don't come to a country with a reputation for using them as clay pigeons. The Shell people are pulling out because Miguelito keeps upping his share of the ante; and the Beards keep blowing up the pipelines and the refineries. Coffee and sugar plantations can't make money at the market prices and pay The Generous Benefactor his cut—"

"In short, a major screw-up?"

"Plus a few minor ones. Another thing: Your foreign editor ever give you the house rules for operating in Latin America?"

" 'Don't criticize the country, and let the dames alone?' "

"Right. Substitute *ruin* for *criticize*, and you've got what El Indominable fractures every day. Both clauses."

"I see," Peter said.

"The funny part about it is he doesn't even like dames—not really. Just uses 'em to get even."

"Even for what?" Peter said.

"Isabel. Old Hundred Thousand. Hell of a note to have that

for a mother. I think that's what kind of drove El Benefactor Generoso off his nut. You know how he came to power?"

"No," Peter said.

"The Big Fish down here backed him. Notably one Manuel Miraflores. Figured this young, ambitious punk would be the perfect weapon against his own class. So Miguelito rose from a small-time *chulo*—pimp is as close to that as you can get in English—petty mobster, strongarm man to Head of the State. Have to admit he was a pretty smooth article, even as a kid. Knew how to ape the manners, speech, and dress of his betters. But the Big Fish forgot one thing."

"Which was?"

"Isabela. They might set up a straw dictator to operate behind, but their brides weren't starting to sit down at a table with the Ex-Star Performer of the exhibitions at The Blue Moon. So, socially, the deep freeze set in. His Nibs has never married, because my guess is he prefers little boys or even lap dogs to babes. And years ago he shipped the kid sister out of the country to keep Old Hundred Thousand from teaching her womanish tricks."

"I heard she's back now," Peter said. "At least according to that idiot Jacinto, she is."

"Yep. I've seen her once or twice. Down here they make jokes about her looks; but I think she's kind of cute. Pert and perky, if you get what I mean. Homely little phiz, but appealing. Keeps to herself—trying to avoid getting hurt, I suspect. His Nibs had her husband knocked off for plotting against him. The point is, Petie, that old Cienmil officially became First Lady. And las Damas Ilustres de la Alta Sociedad weren't having any. The result was that Miguelito got his back up, made his half-brother—maybe—Luis Sinnombre, Head of the Secret Police, and started in to be a real dictator instead of a straw one. Insulting Isabel changed overnight from being High Society's favorite indoor sport to a pastime that would make bullfighting look like croquet. Miguel has filled up three concentration camps with types who said something that even could be mistaken for a lack of respect for that wicked old broad. And the dames—the caper he figured out to cut them down to size, you'd—Oh, hell! Now what?"

Peter turned. The headwaiter was flying toward the table, bowing from the waist from twenty feet away.

"Señor Reynolds," he got out, "there are two reporters from the national newspaper, *El Líder Glorioso*. They wish to interview you and take some pictures, if you don't mind . . ."

"You mean to stand there with your bare face hanging out and imply he could refuse even if he wanted to?" Tim said. "Horse business, Martinez! People get shot for less than that down here."

"It would be a very great honor, Señor Reynolds," the headwaiter said, "which would lend great light to our establishment——"

"Oh, hell—all right," Peter said.

When they had gone, after having taken dozens of pictures of Peter in the act of talking to Tim and the staff reporter of *The Glorious Leader*, Tim sat there, staring at Peter.

"Now you're going to get it," he said.

"Get what?" Peter said.

"The treatment. You're ripe for it. Hell, you're spoiling for it."

"Tim, what the ever-loving hell—"

"Is the treatment? Simple. It's—why should I tell you? Be more fun watching you lapping it up. Tell me, how long is Judy going to be in Vince Gomez's hemstitching emporium?"

"Vince is going to try to keep her there a month. Says he wants to build her up. Claims that if she comes out in a weakened condition, in this climate, she'll catch something godawful, sure as hell."

"He's got something there. A month, eh? Then they've got time."

"Goddamnit, Tim! Who's got time?"

"Miguelito and Company. You ever spend a longish stretch in Costa Verde before?"

"No. A week was my longest up until now. I was down here photographing the Standford Expedition's return from Ururchizenaya. Bringing in my sweetheart, that god-awful, beautiful pre-Columbian statue they call the Goddess of Death. Love that girl. Wish I could bring her back to life. Have you seen it? It's in the Museum of Archeology, here. I go down there twice a week to look into that face. Can't figure how a thing can be so beautiful and so terrible at the same time. Find myself talking to her. You have seen it, haven't you?"

"Yes—and it gives me the creeps. You've got some funny tastes, boy. But tell me, can you figure why this dump has the best press of any country in South America?"

"No. It ought to have the worst. Yet you're right. Everybody sent down here comes home raving about it. And sends home the most nauseatingly saccharine reports about it, and His Nibs. Hell, Tim—you mean he brainwashes them?"

"Something like that. But subtly. He wins friends and influences people."

"But how, Tim? How?"

"Said I wasn't going to tell you. But here's one teensy-weensy lil' hint, amigo. Five'll get you ten that before to-night some dame you never heard of will ring you up. And that just her voice over the telephone will start you climbin' up the wallpaper—"

"And then?"

"You figure it out, Peter Pan," Tim said.

7.

That night, after visiting hours—during which Judith had displayed her really considerable histrionic talent by wringing the last drop of pathos out of the role of the martyred saint, thereby convincing Peter that she was out of danger, because when Judy started acting, he was wryly aware, normalcy was once more at hand—he went back to the flat.

He let himself in with his key and sat down before the typewriter. He wrote steadily until eleven o'clock, grinding out those colorless and neutral stories he'd already found out were the only kind he could get out of Costa Verde, where there wasn't supposed to be any censorship, but where, actually, it was absolute. But, at eleven o'clock sharp—at which ungodly hour Costa Verdians, like all Spanish-speaking peoples, sit down to their heaviest, most important meal—he stopped typing or else, as he knew damned well, the people in the apartment below his would start banging on their ceiling with a broom handle. He sat there, the palms of his hands behind his head, looking out the window. Southward, the sky was strangely red, so he got up and went to the window. Looking out, he could see what the red glow was. Zopocomapetl was acting up again, sending a livid tongue of flame straight up into the night sky. This could, with only a little exaggeration, have been called a major eruption. From the photos published at the time of the last real outburst, five years ago, or at least from his memory of them, Peter judged that this show was only a little smaller than that one had been, but he couldn't really tell, because there weren't any towns like Chitimaya left for old Zopo to bury. There was, of

course, the Indian village of Xochua, where Pepe had died;
but it was on the far side of the volcano, the side where, up
until now, lava had never been known to spill over the cone.
So Zopocomapetl's capacity for destruction was limited, unless
it exerted itself and took care of Ciudad Villalonga, as it had
two hundred years ago, when Costa Verde was still a Spanish
colony and the capital had been called Antigua. But there
wasn't much chance of that, because after the volcano had
wiped out Antigua, the surviving colonists had moved the
capital much closer to the sea, preferring to face their human
enemies, the English buccaneers, than to live under the per-
petual threat of fiery death. Peter stood there watching the
natural fireworks until their sinister beauty palled on him.
Then he turned and started back to his desk, but before he
got there, the telephone rang.

"Señor Reynolds?" the voice said.

"Yes," he said. "Speak."

"You are Señor Reynolds, aren't you?" the voice said. It
didn't purr. It was curiously harsh. But its enunciation was
beautifully crisp.

"Unless somebody gave my mother the wrong package a
long time ago, I am," Peter said.

"Good!" the voice said.

Peter didn't say anything.

"Are you there?" the voice said.

"Yes," Peter said. "And Tim was wrong. Dead wrong."

"I beg your pardon?"

"I said my friend Tim was wrong," Peter said. "He in-
formed me that when you called, your voice alone would
melt the sidewalks. Instead you have the voice of a daughter
of family, who has spent all her life under the teaching of
nuns . . ."

She sighed.

"You are right and he is wrong," she said, "but I wish
sincerely it were vice versa."

"Why?" Peter said.

"Because I should like for you to do a thing for me which
you might if I had the kind of voice he said. Or, more se-

curely if I were the kind of woman who possessed such a voice. But, no—if I were to try to induce you to aid me by giving you the impression I were a beautiful and sensual woman, you would only be disappointed and might even refuse to help me—"

"Then I take it that you are neither beautiful nor sensual?" Peter said.

"I—" she began, and stopped. Then, "Courage, Niña!" she whispered, apparently to herself.

"I am listening," Peter said.

"If one were charitable," she said, "one might call me plain."

"And if one were truthful?" Peter said.

"Ugly," she said. "Perhaps not repugnant; but ugly enough."

"There are differences of opinion. And of tastes there is nothing written. Perhaps I should find you lovely."

She sighed again.

"No," she said, "that is not possible. In the first place, I am very thin. If one bothers to look twice, one can see that I am a woman. I have been told that it is not worth the bother."

"Who told you that?" Peter said.

"My husband," she said. "My late husband, who is dead."

"Oh," Peter said. "And your face?"

"Have you been to the Museum of Archeology here in Villalonga City?"

"Yes," Peter said. "Why?"

"There is a female statue there, brought from the lost city of Ururchizenaya. Since we know nothing of the language of the ancient Tluscola-Toltec civilizations, we do not know what it represents. But, from its aspects of sadness, its look of emaciation, the museum authorities have decided to call it the Goddess of Death. Have you seen it?"

"Yes," Peter said. "It is absolutely gorgeous."

"Oh!" she said.

"*Oh* what?" Peter said.

"Now I cannot make the comparison I was going to."

"Why not?"

"Because now it will seem both false and vain. I was going

to say that if you have seen the so-called Goddess of Death, you have seen very exactly—my face."

"Then, Señora, you are one of the loveliest women on earth," Peter said.

"No, no! Oh, but this is wrong! I start out to demonstrate to you my utter sincerity, because the matter is too important to be deranged with lies, and you—"

"I do not doubt your sincerity, Señora. I merely beg to differ with your opinion and your taste. Say my own is odd. I prefer an interesting face to a beautiful one."

"All right," she sad. "I have been called that. You could legitimately call me interesting. Please, Mr. Reynolds—"

"Ah, one moment!" Peter said. "There is one other detail we must clarify."

"And that is?"

"That of your sensuality."

She didn't answer him at once. And, when she did, her voice, speaking, was very quiet. "That, Señor Reynolds, is a matter between me and my father confessor, and ultimately —my God," she said.

"Bravo!" Peter said.

"Why bravo, Señor Reynolds?"

"I like spirit, and you have it," Peter said.

She was silent a long moment. Then she said:

"All right. I have gone thus far; I might as well go all the way. Señor Reynolds, would you have the kindness to meet me somewhere—tonight?"

"I should be delighted," Peter said.

"Oh!" she said.

"Why Oh! Señora?"

"I—I didn't expect you to say yes. I—I only tried this because I was desperate, and now—"

"And now, two final details. When and where?"

"At the end of the Street of the Fifth of May. Where it runs into the Botanical Gardens."

"That's isolated enough. Even romantic."

"Please, Señor Reynolds, do not entertain ideas. It is not my intention to—"

"I know it is not, Señora. I have lived in Latin America many years."

"Meaning?"

"That girls with cultivated voices like yours don't proposition men. They don't have to. Only one thing puzzles me: You sound extremely young, and yet you say you are a widow—"

"I married at eighteen, Señor. I was married three years. My husband was killed in an airplane crash one year ago."

"Making you all of twenty-two. Now I understand. May I belatedly extend my condolences?"

"Thank you," she whispered. "You are very kind."

"Now, where are we? I am to meet you—?"

"*Al final de la Calle del Cinco de Mayo—*"

"Say that again?"

"At the end of the Street of the Fifth of May."

"Ah, yes. I thought that was what you said. At what time?"

"At midnight." Her voice was so low he could scarcely hear it.

He looked at his watch. "In twenty minutes, then?" he said.

"Sí, Señor."

"One moment! Don't hang up! How am I to know you?"

"You will take a taxi. Before you reach the end of the street get out and dismiss the cab. Walk straight ahead. A car will draw up beside you. A white convertible. I shall be driving it. That is all."

"But how will you know me?"

"I have been following you everywhere you have gone for the last few days," she said. "By now I can distinguish your walk in total darkness."

Peter laughed.

"You find this diverting?" she said.

"My dear young lady," Peter said, "I think you have been seeing too many motion pictures . . ."

"Perhaps. But this of secrecy is very necessary. You will come, won't you?"

"But of course!" Peter said.

He had no sooner put the phone down than it rang again. He picked it up, said:

"Now look, Infant!"

"You are mistaken, Señor Reynolds," a man's voice said.

"You've got something there, friend," Peter said.

"Mr. Reynolds, I am the secretary of His Excellency Señor Corona, Minister of Information and Tourism. His Excellency requests the honor of your presence at a banquet at his residence tomorrow night. Will you be able to attend?"

"Of course," Peter said. "Please convey my thanks to His Excellency. Does the occasion require formal dress?"

"To the extent of a smoking jacket," the secretary said. "The time is eleven o'clock. I may assume that you will come unaccompanied since this of the unfortunate accident of Miss Lovell?"

"You may assume that, yes," Peter said. "If it is not an indiscretion, may I know why you ask?"

"Oh, we have a very pleasant custom here in Costa Verde. When a gentleman is alone, we provide him with feminine company. Exceedingly charming company—"

"From The Blue Moon?" Peter said.

"Why, Mr. Reynolds!" The Secretary's voice sounded genuinely shocked.

"Sorry," Peter said. "I just wanted to know where I stood."

"Your company," the Secretary said, "will be a young married woman whose husband is temporarily absent upon a diplomatic mission. She is a descendant of one of the founders of the Republic. I do not think you will find anything undesirable in her general culture, her manners, deportment, or her morals, Mr. Reynolds. It is not our intent to insult you."

"I beg your pardon most humbly," Peter said. "I was laboring under a misapprehension."

"Quite all right," the secretary said. "Anything else you'd like to know?"

"Yes. Can she count up to five?"

"I—I'm afraid I don't understand," the secretary said.

"Don't worry about it. She will," Peter said.

He hung up the phone, and sat there studying all the things that were wrong with that second call. The hour? No, the hour was all right. Even in private homes, nobody ever ate dinner earlier than eleven o'clock at night in most of Latin America. But to call him only one day ahead of time—that was wrong. Even to call him at all was wrong. For a banquet at a Minister's house, requiring evening dress, nothing less than a formal, printed invitation fitted the circumstances. And, last of all, that pleasant custom the Minister's secretary had mentioned. That was worse than wrong; in any country where Spanish is spoken, that was incredible. A single girl—would have been barely possible. A niece or daughter of the Minister, himself, graciously offering the hospitality of the house under Papa's damned watchful eye —that, maybe, yes. But a married woman whose husband was absent? That no. The Moors hadn't stayed in Spain eight centuries for nothing. And the Conquistadores had imported their temperament to the New World, intact. To put one's bride out to pasture—and on such a loose rein? Not just *no* —*hell no* fitted that one.

"That one," Peter muttered, "stinks on ice!"

Then he looked at his watch and grinned a little.

"Time to start your treatment, Son," he said.

When he saw the car coming toward him, he whistled a little. It was enormous. It drew up alongside him and stopped. Lincoln Continental. The very latest model. Snow white. She had the top up. But even so, the only thing she could have possibly used to attract more attention would have been a flashing red dome light or a police siren. He opened the door and slid in beside her. When the door opened, the automatic roof light came on. But it was set too far back for him to see much of her face. But even in that brief winking on and off of the light, he had the impression that he had seen that strangely regal little head before. Then it came to him he had. In the Museum. That achingly exquisite pre-Columbian head. The likeness was startling.

"*Buenas noches, Señor Reynolds,*" she said. without the

telephone to distort it, her voice was something. It was a true contralto. Speaking, it made interesting atonalities, like modern music.

"*Buenas noches,*" Peter said.

She touched the accelerator. The car moved off. He saw that even the instrument lights were out.

"Would you mind telling me your name?" he said.

"I am very sorry," she said.

"That's a hell of a name," Peter said.

"Please, Señor Reynolds—it is much better that you do not know my name . . ."

"Why?" Peter said.

She sighed.

"Could you not be sufficiently gentlemanly to accept my word that there are excellent reasons for my not telling you who I am?"

"Put that way, I have to," Peter said, "but don't push my rather insufficient gentlemanliness too far, *Muñeca*. It may not be functioning well tonight . . ."

"*Muñeca,*" she said. "Doll. Good. You may call me that. It will serve as a form of address."

"I could think of others," Peter said, "without half trying."

"Please!" she said.

She swept the big car expertly through a whole series of outlying streets. Peter could see that she was taking him out of town, but by a route that avoided every decent neighborhood, every fashionable street.

"You should have used a smaller car," he said, "of a cheaper make. Painted black."

"I thought of that. But it would have caused surprise at home. They know how fond I am of this one."

"But it does not cause surprise for you to leave the house at midnight—alone?"

"I have been married, you know," she said.

"That makes a difference?"

"Yes," and the note of bitterness was there in her voice; "since physically it is impossible to lose one's virginity twice, they are—less concerned, say. I believe they think I am engaging in a romance. And, since they would be delighted to have me marry again—"

"But you, *Muñeca,* would be less delighted?"

And now her voice became ashes and sand.

"My experience of matrimony would not incline me to repeat the experiment, Señor Reynolds. Ah. Here we are . . ."

She swung the big car off the road into a rutted wagon trail that disappeared under a black and menacing grove of trees. Brought it to a stop. Cut the ignition. It was absolutely lightless in there. He could not see her at all.

"Would you like a cigarette?" he said. But instead of saying *un cigarrillo,* which is correct wherever Spanish is spoken, he used the racier Madrid expression *un pitillo.* But she didn't hesitate.

"No thank you," she said.

"You don't smoke, then?"

"Yes, I smoke; but to light a cigarette would enable you to see my face. And it is far better that you do not know too precisely how I look. For the same reason, I ask you please not to smoke."

"I don't smoke. I merely carry cigarettes as bait."

"Oh," she said. "Señor Reynolds—you said that you had been warned that I would call . . ."

"No. I said that I had been warned that a woman would call. And that when she did, just her voice would melt rocks. A part of what is known locally, I'm told, as The Treatment."

"Your information—was accurate, Señor Reynolds."

"Look, *Muñeca,* I like you. In fact, I think you're wonderful. So let's climb down out of this Hitchcock thriller and relax. For instance, call me Peter, will you?"

"Of accord—Peter. It is a nice name. It suits you. Pedros are generally nice."

"Is this part of The Treatment, *Muñeca?*"

"No—Peter," she said. "Please listen to me very carefully, and try to understand what I say. Because I cannot be too explicit. I do not dare."

"Shoot," Peter said.

"All right. You will receive an invitation to a party at the home of a personage high in the government."

"I already have. Five minutes after you called."

"Oh!" she said. "Did they mention an intention to provide company for you?"

"Yes," Peter said.

"They would!" she said. "Since your—your mistress was obliging enough to play into their hands by cutting her silly throat!"

"*Muñeca*," Peter said.

"Sorry. That wasn't nice of me, was it? Strange that I dislike her so! But no matter. Did they tell you who your company was to be?"

"No—beyond mentioning that she was the wife of a diplomat absent upon a mission."

"*Oh, los cabrones! Los cerdos! Los—*"

"*Muñeca*, I felicitate you. Your vocabulary is extremely ladylike."

"I am sorry, Peter. I did not know those words until I married. I learned them from my husband. Listen, I will tell you what will happen. But first, let me say that Roberto is quite unlikely to return from that mission."

"Go on," Peter said.

"And that you will find Marisol extremely attractive. No, you will find that she is one of the most beautiful girls in all Costa Verde—"

"You're making me impatient," Peter said.

"That was what I was afraid of. Additionally, she will be most attentive. She will seem truly impressed by you, even—"

"Swept off her feet by my fatal charm?"

"Exactly."

"But the catch, I gather, is that word *seem?*"

"I do not truly understand this expression *catch*, but if you mean the *trampa*, the trick, you are right."

"Go on," Peter said.

"She will ask you to take her home."

"And?"

"Once you arrive, she will invite you in for a nightcap."

"Then?"

"Then it depends upon you, Peter. I hope you will say to her, 'No thank you, my dear; it is very late'—"

"And if I don't say that?"

She was silent for a long, slow time. Then she said:

"You are a man of the world, Peter. You know what will happen next."

"But, beyond that. Does friend husband come rushing in, waving a revolver? Or does some busy photographer pop up with a flash gun to make interesting pictures? In other words—blackmail?"

"An unmarried man with no official connection with his own government is hardly vulnerable to blackmail, Peter. You have not been discharged from your newspaper because of your liaison with Miss Lovell. And surely that is not the world's most closely guarded secret!"

"Strange how that subject offends you," Peter said.

"While I was following you about, playing my childish and silly game of private detective, I—it seems to me—came to know something about you. At first you seemed to me a hulking brute—"

"Why thanks, *Muñeca!*"

"Hear me out. Then I saw that your mouth contradicted totally your face of an old boxer, which is not so much ugly as battered. And your eyes are the eyes of someone else— of another man entirely."

"What sort of man, Infant?" Peter said.

"The sort who should never, never, never belong to women like Judith Lovell!"

"Nor to your friend Marisol?"

"My friend Marisol does not want you!"

"And you, of course, *Muñeca*—even less?"

He heard the sharp intake of her breath. Then she was silent. Intensely silent.

"*Muñeca*—"

"Yes, Peter?"

"Have I offended you?"

"No, Peter. *You* could never offend me.'

He sat there without moving. Because very exactly what she said was: "No, Peter; *jamás podrías tú ofenderme.*" Switching deliberately from the formal *Usted* to that *tú* which in Spanish, on the lips of a woman like this one, has both the sound and the quality of a caress. You could render *tú* in English as *thou*. But *thou* was wrong. *Tú* is not *thou*. *Tú* is—warmth, and an invitation, and a challenge, and—maybe —even surrender.

"You mean—?" he said.

"Oh, I do not know what I mean! Peter, will you promise me not to—"

"Indulge in fun and games with the lovely Marisol? If you will tell me why not."

She was silent again. Those silences seemed a part of her.

"Why not?" Peter said again.

She went on being silent for a long, long time. Then she said, so softly that he had to bend forward, close to her, to hear it:

"Because I do not want you to." But she didn't say *you*. She went on saying *tú* to him. That quite untranslatable *tú*.

He could feel her breath rustle against his face. It was wonderfully pure and sweet, like a child's. And the position he was in was ridiculous. He was off balance in more ways than one. So he muttered, "What the hell," and put his mouth on hers.

She didn't move. She did not bring her hands up either to embrace him or to slap his face. She lay back against the seat and let him kiss her. Her mouth was unlike any other mouth he had ever kissed. It bloomed on his like the petals of some great, fleshy flower, adhesive, parting, warmsoft, defenseless, tender. Then he felt the wetness on her face. Tasted the salt. At once he drew back.

"I'm sorry," he said.

"Do not be. Peter—"

"Yes, *Muñeca?*"

"Why did you do that? Do you pity me?"

"Jesus H. Christ!" Peter said.

"Do not blaspheme, Peter. Tell me why."

"Does there have to be a why, *Muñeca?*"

"Yes. You have never seen me in the light. You have never spoken to me before an hour ago. Therefore it is not possible for you to love me. And yet you have kissed me—with enormous tenderness. Why, Peter?"

"I love your voice, *Muñeca*," Peter said. "That's one thing."

"And another?"

"I have been to the Museum twenty times to visit that haunting face from another world. I first saw it eight years ago on my first trip to Ciudad Villalonga. Every time I've passed through—if there were time—I've stopped to see her again. I call her my love. The museum guards think I'm crazy, they've caught me talking to her so many times!"

"Oh!" she said.

"So when you said you had her face, I had to come. Only you were wrong."

"I do not have her face, Peter?"

"No. She has yours."

"Oh!" she said again.

"Now it's my turn," he said. "Speaking of whys—why did you *let* me kiss you?"

She was silent.

"*Muñeca*, why did you?"

"I suppose it was because I wanted you to," she said.

"*Muñeca*—"

"No, Peter. You mustn't again."

"Why not?"

"Because it would be wrong. I came out here to save Marisol—"

"From the fate worse than death," he quipped.

"You make a jest of it, but it is very nearly so. Peter, you know the women of our race. Do you believe that one of us would give herself to a man she doesn't even know? Especially when she is very happily married, and adores her husband?"

"I not only do not believe it, I know she would not. Girls of Spanish blood are the most chaste women on earth."

"Thank you for that. Though it is not entirely true. Yet, tomorrow night, that is exactly what Marisol Talaveda will do. Unless you refuse her."

"And if I do refuse her?"

"She—and I—will be most grateful to you."

"*Muñeca,* couldn't you clarify this thing a bit?"

"No, Peter."

"Why not?"

"You are not stupid!" she flared. "Figure it out for yourself!"

"Hmmm—" Peter said. "I take this lovely creature home. She invites me in for a nightcap. Excuses herself to go upstairs and slip into something comfortable: a transparent negligee, say . . ."

"One can see that you have been about," she said. Her voice was tart.

"Of course. But that is, or should be, nothing to you."

"Only it is something to me. I'm sorry! I don't want to seem an aggressive female—"

"Why not? I should love it."

"I know. But I should not."

"Same question: Why not?"

"I—I had a bad marriage, Peter. I have been lonely, too long. And I do not precisely like the ways you appeal to me. They make me ashamed of myself. Now go on with your speculations, and leave me in peace!"

"At the crucial moment, according to you, we are not interrupted. No one takes photographs suitable for French post cards. I simply have a lovely evening and—"

"Go home and write about what a magnificent country Costa Verde is. How *simpatico* the people are. What a bulwark against Communism our Leader is!"

"Now I get it! Tell me, how much does little Marisol get for the job?"

"Ohhh, men! Oh, you!" she said.

"Well?" Peter said.

"Marisol Talaveda de Ruiz Mateos is one of the richest women in Costa Verde in her own right. And the Ruiz, her husband's family, are wealthier still. Hardly the type to assume the role of prostitute, Peter!"

"Then she finds these little outings diverting?"

"Peter, you cannot be this dense!"

"I was teasing you. I know The Leader commands great powers of persuasion. In that regard, would you mind telling me something?"

"If I can," she whispered.

"What has he against Marisol? Why shouldn't he have simply selected some woman of the bad life—a high-class, expensive one, say, instead of forcing a girl of gentle background to—"

She bent her head.

"No answer?" Peter said.

"No. Yes! I shall have to trust you, that's all! I—I do trust you, Peter. All right—it is *because* she is of gentle background. Because when he came to power, the aristocracy scorned him. Because of—because of—his—"

"His mother?" Peter said. "Because of Isabel of the Hundred Thousand Loves?"

"Oh!" she said. "So you know!"

"Yes," Peter said; "that's it, isn't it?"

Her voice was so low that he had to lean close again to hear her.

"Exactly. They would not receive—his mother. Nor—his sister. They said that—that they were unaccustomed to dining with—whores!"

"Isabela, all right. But the sister—is she also?"

"No! In that they were unjust. So, because he is a subtle monster, he set out to reduce their women, their wives, sisters, daughters, to the condition they accused his of. He has nearly succeeded. He *has* succeeded to the extent that now the virtue of all upper-class Costa Verdian women is suspect."

"And the men stand for that?"

"How can they help it? They are, by then, already in prison. And when a woman receives the ring finger of her husband with the wedding ring still on it, packed in cotton wool in a dainty little box, she is—unlikely to refuse her body to the visiting foreigner Miguel feels the real or fancied need of influencing, Peter. Especially since it is not merely a matter of saving one's husband from death, but from death by centimeters prolonged over weeks until usually the mind goes long before the body does . . ."

Peter's voice was very harsh.

"He has—used *you*, thus?"

She looked at him. He could feel her eyes on him in the darkness. "And if he has?" she whispered.

"Nothing," Peter said. "People who voice threats usually don't carry them out. Which is why I don't voice them."

"Oh!" she said. "Peter, about Marisol—"

"That again? You know, *Muñeca*, under these circumstances, I find myself unconvinced of the wisdom of refusing your little friend."

"And I commence to be convinced that you are as swinish as the rest!"

"*Muñeca*, you wound me. Say I refuse her—what happens to her, then?"

"They will force her to try again and again until you succumb, or until it becomes obvious, she is not your type. Then they will send you another light o' love . . ."

"You, for instance?"

"No, Peter; not me. I am not considered attractive enough."

"They're nuts. But, in any event, she has to obey orders, no? If not with me, then with some other foreigner who needs softening up. So why not oblige her and get it over with? Especially if she is as lovely as you said."

"Because, afterward, she will die. By her own hand. I know her. She is the only friend I have. And surely, Peter, you have had enough of that sort of thing!"

"More than enough," Peter said. "But, perhaps you underestimate me, *Muñeca*. Perhaps I can show her so pleasant an evening that this of killing herself will become to her totally unappealing."

She didn't say anything, for a time; then she said slowly: "I—I suppose you could. But, don't you see, that would be worse? That you would have reduced her from the pardonable category of victim to the totally unpardonable one of—adulteress? Oh, Peter, please!"

"Of accord. I will refuse her. But on one condition."

"Which is?"

"That you, *Muñeca mía,* take her place."

She bent her head. He could not see the motion, but he felt it. When she spoke, her voice was infinitely weary.

"No, Peter."

"Why not?"

"Solely because I do not wish you to die," she said.

He heard that *solamente.* Considered it. It had a lovely, lovely sound. He bent, and with only a minimum of groping, found her mouth.

This time, her two hands came up. Her long, slim fingers moved, voiceless and remote in his close cropped hair. Then they dropped to his chest, pushing.

He turned her loose at once.

"For you, *Muñeca,* it would be worth it," he said.

She turned to the wheel, flipped over the ignition key. The motor caught. Purred. When she spoke her voice was humid. He could feel the tears moving through it.

"I will take you home now, Peter," she said.

8.

"Peter—" Judith said.

"Yes, Judy?"

"Can't you take me home now? I feel fine. I feel wonderful. I'm sick of this goddam hospital!"

"No," Peter said.

"Why not?" Judith said.

"Vince won't let me."

"Call him. I'll talk to him. I'll explain it to him."

"You'll explain what to him, Judy?"

"That I can't just lie here and look at you every day, and not do something about it. I can't. I'll go crazy."

"Judy dearest, that is pure, undiluted, unmitigated rot."

"Peter, I can't do without you; I can't!"

"Baby, you did without me a good many years," Peter said.

"But not because I wanted to. I fell in love with you when I was eight. And I never got over it—"

"Which is just another of those weird ideas Dekov should have rid you of."

"It is not! Why . . ."

The nursing sister put her head through the door.

"Señor Reynolds—"

"Yes, Sister?"

"You are wanted on the telephone."

"Peter—" her voice said.

"Yes, *Muñeca?*"

"Have you decided, truly?"

He hardened his voice.

"I told you my decision last night. You must take her place."

"Oh!" she whispered.

"*Muñeca*—"

"Yes, Peter?"

"Would that be so terrible for you?"

She was silent.

"Would it, Infant?"

"What is truly terrible is that it would not be terrible," she murmured; "not at all. Holy Mother, forgive me! What a dreadful thing to say!"

"Then you will?"

"No, Peter."

"Why not?"

"Because afterward, you would die."

"I still say it's worth it."

"And I that you are mad!"

"Over you," he said.

"And I," she said, "for you. Equally. Or worse. Only, what good is it?"

"Good is not the word. I call it great!"

"No, Peter. Because I can never have you. No matter how much I want you. Because neither could I live, knowing I had caused your death."

"Lord!" he said. "There's something morbid about this place."

"Peter—"

"Yes, Infant?"

"Perhaps I shall think of a way. *Adios!*"

He heard the click. The line went dead.

"Who called you? A woman?"

"Yes," Peter said.

"Pretty?"

"Glorious."

"What did she want?"

"What do women always want? You know I can't help it. It's my fatal charm . . ."

"Pe-tah—"

"Oh, brother! Here we go. When my baby starts calling me *Pe-tah,* with that Back Bay accent, head for the woods, men!"

"Peter, is this one of those many truths, spoken in jest?"

"What do you think, Judy?"

"I think you're that barking dog who barks and barks and then takes one hell of a chunk out of where I sit."

Peter lifted the bedcovers, peered under them.

"Hmmn, looks appetizing," he said. "Tasty. You mean you don't trust me, Judy?"

"No. You look too sleek. Too contented. Why, you're fairly purring! *Pe-tah,* are you being unfaithful to me?"

"And if I were?"

"Subjunctive mood, condition contrary to fact. If you *are*, my beamish boy, I'll—"

"You'll what?"

"Cut my neck again. Only deeper."

He went over to the bed. Put his hand under her chin. She was twenty-seven years old now, but without make-up she looked like a child. A rather sweet child, timid and bashful and shy. That quality came through even in her pictures, which made the roles they gave her shocking in a way, to a degree that no other actress could have managed. They had typed her, all right. Whatever the script, what came over from the screen was the portrait of a rather sweet kid engaging in juvenile delinquency without really enjoying it or knowing quite what she was doing. Perked up jaded appetites no end.

"That," he said, "was Don Andres Corona, Ministro de Información y Tourismo. Inviting me to dine *en famille ce soir.*"

"Oh!" she said. "Did you accept?"

"Had to, Judy. You don't refuse invites from bigwigs down here."

"All right. Peter—"

"Yes, Judy?"

"Kiss me."

He kissed her.

"Hmmm—nice! Oh, if I weren't so goddam weak!"

"Good thing you are. Or we'd shock the Sister all to hell," Peter said.

He was tying his bow tie when the doorbell rang. He went to the door, opened it. A policeman stood there. His uniform differed from the ordinary one. It was subdued. Navy blue. His cap had only one thin line of gold braid. Peter had to look very close to see the bulge under his armpit.

"Yes?" Peter said.

"Señor Reynolds?"

"Yes," Peter said again.

"I am your chauffeur. Your car waits below. Don't hurry, Sir. You have plenty of time."

"All right. Mind telling me your name?"

"Enrique," the chauffeur said.

"Very well, Enrique. Wait for me downstairs. I'll only be five minutes more," Peter said.

The car was a Daimler with wickerwork side panels. Peter appreciated the subtlety. A Caddy wouldn't have been enough. A Rolls, too much. A Daimler was just right. Taste; finesse; discretion.

So was the Minister's house. It was a minor miracle as to how all that luxury always stopped one millimeter short of vulgarity.

Peter found himself surrounded. Some of His Excellency's guests tried their English out on him. But when they heard his Spanish, they stopped, relaxed. But not entirely. There was an undercurrent of unease running through that crowd that made the air whine.

Peter looked at the women. Not too directly, which would have been bad form. But they were all clinging to various masculine arms. He saw that the Minister, Señor Don Andres Corona McDowell, was watching the door. He went on watching it out of the corner of his little blue eyes for the better part of half an hour. By a quarter past eleven, he was beginning to sweat a little.

Peter touched his arm, said:

"This of my special company is without importance, Your Excellency. Surely the lady has been unavoidably detained, or even encounters herself indisposed. Tomorrow I shall send her a bouquet of roses with a little note expressing my sorrow at not having had the great privilege of knowing her. But certainly Your Excellency has no reason to be concerned . . ."

But His Excellency's red Celtic face had split into a broad smile under his bushy guardsman mustache.

"Oh, no, my dear Reynolds," he said in English. "Little Marisol is most dependable! Here she comes now—"

Peter didn't follow Don Andres in his rush toward the

door. He stood back and studied Marisol Talaveda, Señora de Ruiz. And immediately revised his estimation of Miguel Villalonga. Sent him to the head of the class. Gave him top marks. Miguelito hadn't missed a trick. This wasn't on the level of the Daimler. This exceeded it.

Marisol Talaveda was dressed in black. In one of those simple little black dresses that defy both analysis and copy. That defy anything on earth except the long side of five thousand dollars. Her hair was what the Spanish call *castaño*, which is actually just off-blonde, not quite auburn. She was slender. Her figure was perfect. And everything about her was innocent, almost virginal, implying a purity of mind, of spirit, that must have been damned uncomfortable to live with if one were her husband. To even think of using this grown-up girl child for such a mission required a turn of thought, a subtlety, a refinement of lechery, a warped kind of sensuality that clearly stood on the other side of perversion.

Peter went on watching her until she was close enough for what was going on behind that very nearly perfect poise to reach out and take him by the throat. He saw that pale pink smiling mouth was screaming so that he could almost hear it. That those enormous, velvety blue eyes had long since eclipsed all the joy that there had ever been on earth. That she was studying him, too, but with horrified fascination. As Mary Stuart must have studied the man with the axe.

"Amigo Reynolds," the Minister said, "this is Marisol—"

"Talaveda, la Señora de Don Roberto Ruiz Mateos," Peter finished for him, "who is as lovely as I have been told. No, lovelier. And whose presence would make me the happiest of men, were it not—"

"Oh!" she said. "You do speak Spanish—and beautifully! You didn't tell me that, Don Andres. I might have said something indiscreet!"

"You, my dear Marisol, are the soul of discretion," the Minister said. "But we are interrupting Señor Reynolds.

You were saying that little Mari's presence makes you unhappy? That, my deah fellow, is a hell of a note!"

"I beg your pardon, Your Excellency; but that is not what I said. My exact words were that la Señora's presence would make me the happiest of men, if she could bring herself to realize I only look like a bear. I don't ordinarily eat little girls alive—not even so dainty a morsel as you are, Señora—"

"But you could be persuaded, eh, Reynolds?" Don Andres said.

Peter looked at her.

"In this case, I think not, Your Excellency," he said.

Now she was really looking at him.

"Why?" she said.

He smiled.

"Say the bear's a curiously tender beast—with a finicky appetite. He only dines on grubworms and wild honey. Never upon terrified does, no matter how lovely they are. And that, at least as far as this particular gross animal is concerned, any relationship whatsoever must be based upon mutual consent. And that consent must be real. Don't you agree with me, Don Andres?"

"Perfectly," the Minister said. "If only a few other chaps I know felt the same way about it, what a world we'd have, my friend!"

Sitting beside her, listening to her voice, Peter began to feel contented with life. Her voice was utterly lovely. Low and soft and sweet. She seemed to have formed a genuine liking for him, because her voice was no longer taut with nerves, but rather vibrant with what must have been hope.

"Peter," she said, "you don't mind if I call you Peter, do you? It seems I've known you forever!"

"I'm delighted. But, truthfully, if I can say so without seeming vain, girls usually like me. That is, after they come back from wherever they run screaming to, the first time they see me."

"Strange," Marisol said. "You really aren't ugly, you know.

I think you must have been in a car smash-up. Your nose has been broken, hasn't it?"

"Yes," he said, "but it wasn't a car."

"What was it?" she said.

"A Red Chinese sergeant in charge of interrogating prisoners in Korea. He wanted me to admit I was guilty of bacterial warfare."

"Oh!" she said. "Peter—"

"Yes, Mari?"

"You really *are* nice. Just as she said."

"Just as *who* said?"

"My friend. You've never seen her. And she's forbidden me to tell you her name. But you'll meet her soon. And when you do—"

"When I do meet her, what, Mari?"

"Be gentle with her, Peter, please!"

He grinned at her.

"I'm usually gentle with little girls, Mari. Tell me: Is she as pretty as you are?"

"She—she's not pretty at all, Peter. But I do wish you wouldn't mind that."

"Maybe I won't."

"She's not ugly. Just—just odd-looking. Exotic somehow. Her face is like a tribal mask. If I were a man, I'd find her exciting."

"I do," Peter said.

"What did you say?"

"Nothing. Go on. This of your friend interests me."

"It should. You see, she started—well—investigating you. For—for reasons I'm not free to tell you."

"I know those reasons. I find them hateful. No—nauseous. There was never the slightest danger that I would have gone along with this monstrous charade. To me, there is only one excuse for certain acts, Mari. Love. The kind of love that continues after one has resumed a vertical position. That goes on. Forever."

"Oh!" she whispered. "Oh, she's right! No wonder she's so in love with you!"

"Is she?"

"Yes. I told her she was foolish. That one couldn't love a man one had never talked to, didn't really know. You know what she said to that?"

"No, what?" Peter said.

"That when I met you, I was not to pay any attention to your shoulders nor to your rather brutal face. 'Look at his mouth,' she said; 'then his eyes. You'll see what I mean.'"

"And do you?"

"I think so, yes. Your mouth and eyes are—gentle. Peter, listen to me. She—she's not responsible for the terrible position she finds herself in. She didn't choose her parents any more than you and I chose ours. What I'm trying to say is that she's—so vulnerable. Her life has been—awful. Emilio treated her like dirt."

"Why?"

"She will tell you, one day. It is not my place to. She's so terribly alone. Surrounded by people, sitting upon a mountain of gold; with a terrifying amount of power in her hands, she's alone. Cut off from any happiness, any joy—"

"By her looks?"

"Oh no! By the walls of hate that surround her. Hate she did nothing to cause, but cannot cure—"

"Maybe I can kick those walls down for her," Peter said.

After dinner, which Peter remembered as having been absolutely marvelous without being able to recall a single thing he had eaten, they danced. Marisol was a beautiful dancer. She floated, two full centimeters off the floor. But she had gone away from him, somehow. Her small, sweet face was remote. Then abruptly, nervously, she said:

"Would you mind taking me home, Peter? I'm very tired."

He stared at her. "Of course," he said.

He saw at once that excuses were unnecessary. That everyone at the party had been expecting this. The women looked contemptuous. The men hard-eyed, grim. So he made his excuses anyhow, in person, and in form. Then he took Marisol by the arm and led her out to the car.

Enrique jumped out at once to open the door for them. They got in. The Daimler moved off. Marisol didn't say anything to Peter. She didn't even sit close to him. She seemed to have forgotten that he existed. Peter sat beside her and watched the quivering rolls of flesh on the back of Enrique's neck.

The car swept up a curved driveway under the palms, the tamarinds, the lavenders. The house was buried under dark masses of bougainvillea, hibiscus, frangipani.

Enrique got out, held the door open for them.

Marisol looked at Peter. Her smile was something to see. "Would you care for a nightcap, Peter?" she said.

"Look, Mari," he began, "it's awfully late, and—"

But her hand came out and took his. Her nails bit into his palm. She closed one gorgeous blue eye, suggestively.

"Please, Peter," she said.

He stood there. His lips moved, soundlessly: "Must I?"

She nodded vigorously. Her face was very white.

He made up his mind, said the only thing that could be said:

"All right," and added under his breath: "Judy baby— I think my will power's up to par, but if it isn't, or if what they're holding over this lovely child's head is too goddam rough, will you forgive me, please?"

"What did you say?" Marisol said.

"A prayer. One I don't think is going to be answered. And I find I need that nightcap."

Her voice, speaking, made a flute note.

"You needn't wait, Enrique," she said.

It was beautifully planned. She poured excellent smoky Scotch over the ice cubes. Said, pleasantly:

"Amuse yourself, Peter, while I go upstairs and slip into something cool."

"Now look, Mari!" he began; but she clamped a slim hand over his mouth. When she took it away, he whispered: "The servants?"

She nodded, swiftly. Said, her voice high, taut, bright:
"Oh, I'll be right back, Peter." And ran up the stairs.

He waited. Then he saw her coming back down again.
She hadn't changed. She still had on that wonderful little
black dress. He had already opened his mouth to say "Now,
what the hell?" when he saw that he was wrong; that she had
changed totally. That the woman in that black dress wasn't
Marisol Talaveda de Ruiz at all.

He stood up, watching her come down those stairs step
by step by step like a dream figure, slowly. And now, seeing
her in the light for the first time, everything he had guessed
about her, every intuition was confirmed. She was thin. Thin
enough to wear that dress like a professional model, wear it
in a way that Marisol couldn't have worn it, or any other
woman he had ever known. Her face was a Greco, even to
the distortion along the vertical planes, even to that curiously exciting cool-toned hint of—green? blue? greenish-
blue?—in the shadows. Only Bernard Buffet had brought it
up to date, because El Greco would never have conceived
the totally nonethereal quality of that mouth. That mouth.
Too wide-lipped, full, defenseless, tender, wounded unto
death for her inhollowed tribal fetish of a face. Nine men
out of ten would have found her ugly, he knew. But now,
here, at that instant of time, in that particular place, he,
Peter Reynolds, was that lonely tenth man. He found her
glorious.

He stayed there looking at her, watching the play of light
and shadow over that sculptured mobile of a face as she
came down those stairs in the midst of velvety silence, un-
breathing still, watching him out of those enormous, long-
lashed, definitely slanting eyes, turning toward him the face
which—even under the short black cap of hair, a gamine's
cut that on her defined the word *chic* and was actually
closer-cropped than most men's—could have played An-
tigone or Electra or Phaedra or even Medea without a mask.

He couldn't stop looking at her. He stared at her openly,
frankly, almost rudely, peering into that wonderful, haunt-

ing, tragic, tender face, at those eyes of Nefertiti, his gaze caressing the exquisite sculpture of her cheekbones, the long cool slant of jaw, that warhorse flare of nostrils above a mouth that, even smiling, both was and made a wound—until she blurred sight out of focus by too much nearness, going up on tiptoe, tilting that matchless head sidewise, and drawing every hurt he'd ever known, every disappointment, chagrin, anguish, defeat, shame, loss, along with whatever residual scattered, shattered grains of rationality, of will, he had left by then, out through his suddenly, tenderly assaulted mouth.

"*Muñeca*," he said. And then they both heard the muted thunder of that heavy motor, the whining screech of the tires, as it tore by the window in a long blued milk flash, bottoming out with a sodden thump at the end of the driveway, slamming onto the pavement, going on.

"Marisol?" he whispered.

"Yes," she said. "In my car, my clothes, with my passport. Her picture's pasted over mine. Since so very few minor functionaries have ever seen me, it doesn't matter. With a ticket, bought by me personally in her handbag. Flight 201, which leaves in half an hour. She'll make it. There's no traffic this late—or rather this early. And no one will dare stop that car. The ticket's one-way—to New York. So now she's safe."

"And you?" he said.

"And I—I've come to take her place. Wasn't that what you wanted, Peter?"

He stared at her. Speaking now, his voice was rough:

"In every way?" he said.

She smiled. The impact of that warm red curl of lip hit him like a fist.

"In every way," she said.

She kept filling his glass. But that excellent smoky-tasting Scotch might as well have been ice water for all the effect it had. The slow, deep sickness crawling in his middle negated it, killed it, effortlessly. So now she tried another tactic. She took direct action. She came and sat down beside him. Took his face between her two hands, her long slim fingers cool and dry and slight and almost untouching along the slant of his jaw. Then she bent and clung her warm, soft, adhesive mouth to his, forcing his lips apart, exploring the limits of his resistance, his will, with that wine-scald, bitter-honey, hot, sweet, melting serpentine thrust and probe.

Angrily, brutally, he put his hand upon her secret body. She moaned a little, went on clinging her mouth to his while her long fingers worked in the close-cropped iron-gray brush of his hair.

He drew back, said:

"Why?"

Her eyes went blacker still.

"There are no *whys*, Peter," she said.

He looked at her. Said it again. "Why?"

She shrugged.

"I have been without a man too long. I am not of the temperament of a nun. You appeal to me. Simple, no?"

"No," Peter said. "*Muñeca*—"

"Yes, Peter?"

"Put an X beside the proper choice: Prig. Boor. Brute. Insensitive dolt. Or plain damned fool."

She laughed. A long, ice-bright glissando, with the top notes flattened into a haunting dissonance. A bar from Stravinsky, combined with Bartok, say.

"I should put the X beside brute," she said, "but I should be wrong, shouldn't I? Because your mouth contradicts both your jaw and your shoulders, Peter. It is so sensitive that it is practically defenseless. I love your mouth. May I kiss it again?"

"Later," he said. "Now, we talk."

"So?" she said. "What do we talk about, Peter?"

"You. Why you're doing this."

"But I told you. I am a poor starved female who is intrigued by those shoulders. By your look of—of brute male——"